"Don't get in tr[ouble]"

"Ella, I've risked my life for people I will [ ], I've known since you were in grade school." As Owen looked at those lush green eyes, his heart beat to a faster tempo, the pulse thundering loud in his ears. He cleared his throat. "You're my best friend's sister, and my family loves you. Why wouldn't I take a risk for you?"

"Because I don't want you to," she said firmly. "Because this isn't your battle."

"Well I'm making it my battle."

"Why?"

"I just told you."

"No. You could let the police handle it. Family friendship doesn't go this far. Ray would understand."

"No he wouldn't."

She blew out a breath that ruffled her bangs. "You've nearly been run down. Isn't that enough?"

He fought to keep his tone level. "Have we cleared your name yet? Have we gotten back everything you've lost? Your work? Your reputation? Your freedom?"

"No," she said, voice breaking.

"Then I guess you have your answer."

Dana Mentink is a national bestselling author. She has been honored to win two Carol Awards, a Holt Medallion Award and an RT Reviewer's Choice Best Book Award. She's authored more than thirty novels to date for Harlequin's Love Inspired Suspense and Harlequin Heartwarming. Dana loves feedback from her readers. Contact her at danamentink.com.

Books by Dana Mentink

Love Inspired Suspense

Visit the Author Profile page at Harlequin.com for more titles.

TREACHEROUS TRAILS

DANA MENTINK

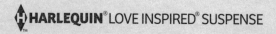
HARLEQUIN® LOVE INSPIRED® SUSPENSE

Recycling programs
for this product may
not exist in your area.

LOVE INSPIRED BOOKS

ISBN-13: 978-1-335-54363-9

Treacherous Trails

www.Harlequin.com

Printed in U.S.A.

Then said Jesus unto his disciples,
If any man will come after me, let him deny himself,
and take up his cross, and follow me.
—Matthew 16:24

To Nancy and Phil, God loving, horse loving,
Kingdom serving souls. Thank you.

ONE

Ella Cahill rubbed her eyes as she climbed behind the wheel of her old van and sipped tea out of her thermos to revive herself. The pounding behind her temples was growing more and more painful. Probably fatigue. Trying to squeeze just one more appointment into her farrier's schedule meant another small step toward covering the monthly bills, but it took a toll. *You can sleep tomorrow* was her motto, but that luxurious day of rest never seemed to come. She rolled down the window halfway, hoping that since the tea hadn't worked, the cold January temperatures would restore her. Sucking in a deep lungful of crisp air, she felt grateful once more for Gold Bar, her sleepy little hometown tucked deep in the heart of California's gold country. Funny how her craving for travel and adventure had mellowed away, leaving quiet contentment behind.

"Done so soon?"

The sudden appearance of Bruce Reed, dark

hair slicked down and smelling of cologne, made her jump. Her skin prickled as her friend Luke's words from earlier in the day came back to her.

Reed's a wolf in sheep's clothing. He's dangerous.

"Yes," Ella said. "I tended to Bellweather. I can't understand how the shoe came loose. I just shod him last week."

Reed shrugged. "Horses are dumb animals. They don't know enough to take care of themselves like we do. Nice of you to make an emergency call."

Dumb animals? Though she knew Bruce Reed was in his fifties, he seemed ageless close up, his skin smooth and tight across his prominent cheekbones, no extra softness anywhere. He quirked a smile to reveal blinding white teeth, the canines pointed and slightly longer than the rest. Wolflike, she mused before she blinked herself back to reality. The fatigue was really getting to her.

She started the engine. "I've got to go, Mr. Reed."

"Call me Bruce. What's the rush?" He stroked her fingers that still clutched the window frame. "Come join Candy and me for a drink."

"No, thank you," she said while easing her hand away. "I don't drink and my sister is waiting." Ella had taken a moment to hurry home in between farrier appointments to be sure Betsy had dinner before they took a walk together. A stab of anxiety twisted through her. If she could just save enough to pay for a nurse to come and check on her sister, help her get the proper exercise for her atrophied muscles… *"Work today, rest tomorrow,"* Ella silently repeated to herself, but her body was screaming for sleep.

Ella blinked as her vision blurred. "I've really got to go," she said, wondering when he would detach himself from her door.

"Take good care of yourself, Ella," he said with one final smile.

She could feel his gaze on her as she drove along the lane away from Candy Silverton's lavish stables on the outskirts of Gold Bar. Without warning, Ella began to shake, her grip loosening from the wheel.

Something was wrong, very wrong. Guiding the van to the shoulder, she patted her pockets for her cell phone but could not pull it free, so she unbuckled and stepped from the van. Fresh air would help. Her thermos fell out, rolling off into the leaves, but she was too unsteady to bend over and retrieve it. Her knees buckled and she fell, hands planted on the ground. All she could do was breathe against the dizziness. Vaguely, from the deepest part of her instincts, she heard someone approaching.

Help me, she tried to call out, but the words remained locked inside. Then she was sliding stomach-first onto the ground, rocks biting into her face, unable to move. From above she detected a presence.

Please, she tried to whisper.

Everything went black as a sack was shoved over her head, rough, smelling of oats, an old feed bag. A scream of terror lodged in her throat. Her arms were pulled behind her. Panic surged, and she tried to kick out, but her limbs were leaden. What was wrong with her? *Something in her system*, her brain thought. No, something in the tea, a drug.

Whoever it was seized her arms and yanked her up. It took her a long moment to realize she was being shoved back into her van, behind the wheel. Something cold made her gasp, a liquid, the sharp scent of alcohol, beer, pouring over her clothes, soaking her flannel jacket, her pants.

Whatever was happening, it was meant to destroy her, she was certain. Her only chance of survival was to get out of that van. She had to force her body to act before it was too late. With every grain of mental strength she readied herself, trying to tense her internal muscles without letting on that she was conscious. She could feel the cool air billowing in through the open van door against her. When he stepped away to close it, she would have one shot, one slender chance, one moment that would decide her fate.

Hands fumbled with her jacket, tugging, then her tormentor reached to straighten her shoulders, posing her as if she were a dime store mannequin. Her mind felt foggy and she was not sure if her eyes would work properly should she manage to get free of the bag. His fingers reached the bottom of the sack and he started to pull it off. She waited no longer.

Arms flailing like unwieldy tree limbs, she catapulted from the car, the burlap falling away. Fingers grasped the back of her jacket so she wriggled out of it and kept on, forcing her legs to carry her toward the trees, anywhere away from her abductor.

Half staggering, half running, like some zombie from a horror movie, she made it to the trees, the sound of pursuit ringing in her ears. Her numb feet caught in a twisted tree root and she tumbled down a shallow ravine in a helpless jumble of arms and legs.

She hit the bottom, the breath driven out her.

Move. Move or he'll find you. All around were spindly pine trees and granite chunks protruding through a carpet of pine needles and fallen tree trunks. She saw a hollow underneath one of the downed trees. Dragging herself there, heart thundering, she crawled in, scooping handfuls of the dead leaves and needles over herself as a form of filthy camouflage. The sound of feet creeping through the needles caused the blood to freeze in her veins. He had to be no more than three yards from her hiding spot.

"Lord, God," she prayed, but she could not finish as a wave of darkness overcame her.

Owen slammed his truck to a halt in the morning sunlight, shocked at the sight of Ella Cahill, the ranch farrier and his childhood friend, crawling out of the shrubs onto the road. In disbelief, he flung the door open and ran to her, ignoring the twang of pain in his damaged leg.

"Ella. What happened? How badly are you hurt?"

She reached out a hand and grabbed his arm, the cold of her fingers seeping right through his shirt sleeve. "Someone…someone abducted me."

He was momentarily speechless. "Who?"

"I don't know. There was…" She touched her face as if searching for something. "He put a bag on my head. I think he drugged the tea in my thermos."

Something inside him went white-hot with anger. "Someone you know?"

"I'm not sure." Her voice was high-pitched, tight. "Where's my van?"

"I didn't see it."

Her eyes scanned the sunlit shoulder of the road before widening. "Owen, what time is it?"

"Six a.m."

Her mouth fell open. "Thursday morning? Betsy's been alone all night?" She struggled to her knees. "I have to get home."

"We need to call the police and an ambulance."

"I don't need an ambulance. Call the police, but get me home first. They can talk to me there, okay? Please?"

Her face was scratched and bruised, red hair matted with burrs and leaves. What kind of person would harm Ella Cahill? He put his rage aside and prioritized the mission. Get her home. Get her help. Punishing her attacker would have to wait.

Easing a hand under her elbow, he helped her stand slowly, gratified that there were no outward signs of broken bones or blood. He wanted to scoop her up and carry her to his truck, but she was already moving in that direction under her own power.

She pushed tangled hair from her face. "How did you know to find me here?"

"I've been driving the area for an hour searching for you." He hesitated. "The cops, Larraby I mean, called the ranch before sunrise looking for you."

"Why me?"

He still could hardly believe it himself. "They got an anonymous call that you and Candy Silverton's nephew, were in an altercation yesterday."

"An altercation with Luke? Who said that?"

"I don't know, but now Luke is apparently missing."

"Missing?" she gasped.

"Yeah, Candy called it in early this morning

when she discovered his bed hadn't been slept in. She's worried he's been in an accident or something."

"And they think I have something to do with that?"

He fisted hands on his hips. "I'm not sure what they think. I wanted to find you and you didn't answer your cell. There was no answer at your home either."

Ella caught her lip between her teeth. "Betsy can't work the phone very well. Owen, please get me home. She will be frantic with worry or she might have fallen. She's not safe getting in and out of her wheelchair by herself. Her ability to walk has really deteriorated."

"We'll be there in fifteen."

She followed him to the driver's-side door, preparing to slide in as he opened it for her until she pointed to a bit of flannel lying half-hidden under a scattering of pine needles.

"There's my jacket," she said, frowning. "It should be near my van."

"I'll get it." He picked it up. Muscles knotted in his stomach as he examined it.

"Is my phone in the pocket?" Ella called.

"No phone." He held the jacket closer for her to see. Using the edge of the sleeve, he pulled something from her breast pocket—a broken farrier's rasp.

The edge was covered in blood.

His gaze caught hers and he knew her mind screamed with the same question.

Whose blood was it?

TWO

Ella tried to focus on Owen as he drove to her house. Strong face, wide cheekbones, the face of a model beneath the hat, not the cowboy he was or the marine he had been. She knew he was holding back a million questions, but she had no answers for any of them. Who had taken her? She remembered what Luke told her about Bruce Reed. *He's dangerous*. Her gut told her the same thing but she had not seen her attacker's face, heard his voice. Reed had no reason to harm her. Where was her van? How had her farrier's rasp gotten bloody? And the question that kept stabbing at her insides…where was Luke Baker?

Instead of succumbing to hysteria, she focused on the details as she tried to piece together the story for Owen. His presence was comforting, the worn knees of his jeans, his free hand brushing her wrist, eyes like stonewashed denim that flicked over her face, crew cut hair grown out now into a crown of blond that scattered across his forehead. Owen Thorn, the man she'd known since she was seven, a fixture in her life until the day he'd deployed. Just three years older than her, but he'd assumed the role of big brother over the years until he gave himself to the marines. And now here they were again, Owen standing in for her brother Ray.

She gripped his offered fingers.

His mouth tightened. "Ella, I don't think… I mean, I'm just asking because the police will. Were you…have you been drinking?"

Blinking hard, she raised her chin. "No," she said in a voice louder than she meant, snatching her hand away from his touch. "He poured it over me, whoever it was. If I can figure out where it happened, there will be proof. The burlap sack, the bottle he was holding. My thermos. I think it might have been Bruce Reed. He was the last one I saw before I left Candy's ranch."

"It's not the time to work all that out. Let's get you home."

"As long as you know I wasn't drinking," she insisted.

Owen had no doubt heard from her brother Ray, his best friend, of her wild rebellion during their first deployment. But that was the past. *Forgiven, forgiven, forgiven*, she chanted silently, but her cheeks went hot with shame that Owen would even suspect such a thing.

"We'll check on Betsy. I can ask my mom to

come and stay with her while we go talk to the cops," he said.

Anger still simmered in her belly at the doubt she imagined she'd heard in his voice. What right did he have to judge her? Especially when she hadn't done anything wrong...this time. But where had the blood come from? Her mind was foggy from the time she'd left Reed at Candy Silverton's stables to the moment she'd crawled out of the ravine. There had to be proof that she was telling the truth.

"I have to find my van."

"After I get you settled, I'll go look for it."

"No." Whatever it was, whatever she'd done, she would take care of it herself. Betsy counted on her. There would be no more painful moments with Owen Thorn, a man who didn't believe her. "I'll find it myself."

"Not in that condition, you won't," he commanded, as if she was a new recruit.

"Owen..." She started to retort, but pain made her break off, clapping her hands to her temples.

He let out a long, slow breath and she could feel his gaze wandering her face. "Oh, Ella Jo," he breathed in a voice so gentle it broke her heart.

"Don't call me that," she said. Tears pricked her closed eyes. "That was a lifetime ago and I'm not seven years old anymore."

When he parked, she flung open the door and ran for the house, calling out for her sister.

* * *

Owen stood on the shadowed front porch, suddenly unsure what to do. A memory washed over him of the three of them, Ella, her brother Ray and himself, swinging on a rope across the creek behind their house, competing to see who could hang the longest before plunging into the icy water. Owen won enough times to infuriate Ray, which in turn sent Ella into gales of girlish giggles before she took her turn and beat them both. They passed the early years of their lives together, morphing from little kids to high schoolers, to semi-adults, the memories clear and sharp.

But now the laughter and innocence seemed to be light-years away. An ominous feeling weighed him down like body armor and he found himself entering, passing through the minuscule kitchen and into the family room where he discovered Ella with Betsy. The knot of tension in his gut loosened a fraction.

As a very young child, Betsy had suffered a brain injury due to some sort of hemorrhage, he knew, though neither Ella nor Ray liked to talk about it. Ella knelt on the braided rug next to her sister's wheelchair, both their faces wet from crying. Betsy was only four years Ella's senior, but she appeared much older.

"I am so sorry I didn't come home last night," Ella whispered, stroking her sister's hand. "You must have been so scared. I was…in an accident."

Betsy clung to Ella's fingers, green eyes a paler shade than her sister's, hair a light auburn instead of Ella's flaming red. Owen did not know how much Betsy understood, but she could see relief in the woman's face, which indicated she'd been plenty worried.

"I'll make you some breakfast right now," she said to her sister. "I know you're hungry."

"I called from the truck," he said quietly. "The police are on their way."

"Have they found Luke yet?"

"No."

She turned those vivid green eyes on him. A shadow darkened their brilliance, fear, and he felt stung by a helpless desire to make it go away. He wished he could take back his earlier question. Ella would not have gone out drinking and left her sister, and even if she had, he was not the one to mete out judgment. *Hypocrite*, his mind jabbed. *Less than a year since you couldn't stop downing painkillers, or have you forgotten?* He went to Betsy.

"Hi, Betsy. I haven't seen you since Christmas Eve." The sisters had attended the annual holiday party hosted by his parents on the Gold Bar Ranch. They all had much to celebrate, since his eldest brother Barrett and his new wife, Shelby, had survived a murder attempt just days before. But all had ended well, and the newly married couple was installed in the ranch pending the completion of the home Barrett was building for her with the family's help.

Ella brought in a plate of scrambled eggs and toast cut into small squares and settled a special utensil in her sister's grip that allowed her better control. The wheelchair was a manual one, with Copper County Hospital stenciled on the back.

Ella flipped her hair away from her face. "The hospital was discarding them. They said I could take it."

He hated that he'd made her have to explain herself. She wasn't a marine under his command, he reminded himself. She didn't owe him anything, including explanations.

Guilt licked at his heart that he'd fallen so far out of Ella's life. But he'd heard rumors of the trouble she'd gotten into before he'd returned stateside. Rumors he'd never bothered to ask her about. Maybe he hadn't wanted to know, preferring the distant memories of lazy summer days spent at the creek.

"I forgot the orange juice," Ella said, scurrying back to the kitchen.

While Betsy ate, he wandered to the window that allowed a partial view of the carport and the sprawling backyard, shadowed by massive pine trees that needed trimming.

He peered closer out the frosted window, his stomach tightening.

"Ella?" he called.

She joined him after she gave her sister the juice and stopped in the bedroom to pull on clean clothes and wash up. He jutted his chin toward the carport.

Her face went pale. "That's…that's my van."

The muscles in his stomach clenched even more, the same way they had just before the quiet streets in Afghanistan exploded with enemy fire.

She stared at the van and he could read the tension. She was slight, petite, barely came up to his collarbone. For some reason, in that moment, she looked even smaller. He laid his hand slowly on her shoulder, delicate under his wide palm.

"Ella," he said quietly. "Tell me everything that happened last night."

Ella swallowed as she stared out the window at the carport. The trees swayed and trembled in the winter wind. A set of birds exploded from the foliage, startled.

"After you left the stables, did you stop anywhere on the way home?"

She rounded on him. "Owen, I know I messed up in the past but I promise you I did not drink anything except the tea in my thermos. It must have been drugged."

"I wasn't implying anything."

"Just go home, Owen. Thanks for the ride, but I'll figure out what to do on my own."

He shifted, taking the weight off his wounded leg, calloused hands on hips. "You need help."

It was suddenly too much. "I needed help four years ago when you deployed right after my brother did. Or maybe when my dad died—maybe that would have been a good time for some help, but you weren't there, and neither was Ray." Her voice wobbled.

He winced as if she'd hurt him. Good. He deserved it for thinking she would go out drinking and leave her sister alone and helpless. *Even though you did exactly that when Ray and Owen deployed.*

"Go home, Owen."

Part of her wanted him to march right on out to his truck and gun it out of the driveway, but another part, a tiny part that she'd hidden away since she was seven years old, wished desperately that he would stay.

"Okay," he said. "If that's what you want."

Owen strolled through the house and out the front door, hesitating just past the threshold. She thought with a moment of warmth that he'd changed his mind. Instead she saw a police car pull up at the end of her driveway. Her mouth went dry.

Officer John Larraby nodded to Ella as he got out of his cruiser and walked up the drive. "Got time for a few questions, I hope," Larraby said. She nodded and Owen moved in closer.

Ella told him everything in a hurried rush of words while Larraby dutifully jotted notes.

"Miss Cahill, Candy Silverton is looking for her nephew, Luke Baker. Were you with him last night?"

Ella blinked. "I spoke to him at the stables in the afternoon when I was shoeing the horses."

"I was told you had a heated argument with Mr. Baker."

"No, I did not," she snapped. "Someone is lying about me and I want to know who."

Larraby cocked his head ever so slightly and dread cascaded along her spine. "What did you talk to him about?"

Should she say it? Repeat what he'd said in confidence? Tell the truth, her gut told her. "He had some...reservations about Bruce Reed, about his intentions toward Candy Silverton. I think you should ask him more about it."

"As I've said, we can't find him, but we did find something else in the woods outside Silverton's stables."

Again, the tremor of dread. "What?" she forced herself to ask.

"Blood," he said. "And lots of it."

Owen watched the color drain out of Ella's face until her freckles stood out in stark relief against her milk white skin. Shock, he recognized. He'd seen it in the faces of his marine brothers when they'd taken a round, the befuddled look of a body trying to process that it had just been shot. He grabbed her hand and she let him, fingers small though calloused and tough from her work as a farrier. "Ella," he said quietly. "You're not talking anymore until there's a lawyer present."

"A lawyer?" she repeated dully. "Owen, I didn't do anything to Luke. He's my friend."

"A friend you borrowed money from?" Larraby asked.

Her face went from cream to plum. "I...yes. I did." She looked at the floor. "He offered to loan me five hundred dollars to have Betsy's wheelchair fixed. I was going to pay him back by the end of the month."

Oddly, Owen felt a twist of jealousy. She hadn't come to him for a loan? She'd gone to some other guy when it was his duty to Ray to help her in any way he could? Duty. Maybe she didn't want to be anybody's duty, wanted to stand on her own two feet just as badly as he did. Still, he wanted to snap at her to keep away from the spoiled, soft-handed Luke Baker.

"Mr. Reed said Baker complained that he wanted the money repaid and you weren't cooperating," Larraby said.

"Bruce Reed is lying," she spat, irises sparking.

Larraby wrinkled his nose and raised an eyebrow. "Have you been drinking, Miss Cahill?"

"No," she said through gritted teeth.

"Are you sure about that?"

"Yes," she hissed. "I already explained that."

He pursed his lips. "Okay. Would you mind letting me take a look at your vehicle?"

"Got a warrant?" Owen said. "Otherwise she doesn't have to show you squat."

Larraby's look was poisonous. He and Owen's youngest brother, Keegan, were biological half siblings, though their father would not acknowledge Keegan. Owen's parents adopted Keegan at age sixteen. Bad blood boiled between Larraby and Keegan, and spilled over into the rest of the Thorn family. Probably always would.

"Of course you can see my van," Ella said, stepping inside to snatch her keys off the table. "Here's my spare set."

"Ella," Owen said, pulling her close and talking low, his lips brushing the shell of her ear. Everything in him was screaming a danger message, loud as the whine of an incoming rocket. "Don't." But she was already pushing away, following Larraby to the back of the house to the carport.

Larraby strolled around the vehicle slowly, examining every inch of the white metal exterior. He gestured to the driver's-side door handle. "May I?"

"Yes," she said.

"No," Owen replied at the same moment.

Larraby gave Owen the whisper of a smile. *You lose,* it said.

Above all things, Owen detested losing, always had.

And Larraby knew it.

Larraby unlocked the door with the key and swung it open, bending to peer inside. After a moment he straightened.

"See?" Ella said with a sigh of relief. "I don't have Luke bound and gagged in my van, okay? I will do everything I can to help you find him, but I did not harm him in any way."

Larraby nodded. "I'll make a note of that, but before I go, one more thing. I'm going to open up the back, if you don't mind."

Ella nodded and Larraby unlocked the rear doors of the old van. Owen had heard from Ray that Zeke Potter, Ella's mentor and the town veterinarian had sold it to her. Ray didn't approve of the transaction, since every weekend it seemed his sister reported she was under the hood, repairing something in the aged engine, but Owen suspected she enjoyed that part. She was as at home with engines as she was with horses. A heavy wire grate separated the driver's area from the back, ideal for housing the collection of rasps, nippers, hammers, nails and other paraphernalia of her trade, neatly stowed.

Larraby was leaning into the van. After a moment, he turned, his expression hard as stone. "I'd like to hear you explain this one." He stepped aside. Ella cried out in horror. She and Owen stared into the sightless eyes of Luke Baker.

THREE

Owen grabbed her when she shot back, slamming into his chest. He could feel the quick shuddering breaths that shook her. "It's all right," he wanted to say, but nothing about the situation was all right.

Luke Baker's blond head protruded from under the blanket at an awkward angle. Owen had seen death plenty of times before and although Larraby checked for a pulse, there was zero chance that the man was alive. His eyes were open, staring and dull, a splash of dried blood visible on his neck above the wool blanket where the tip of a broken farrier's rasp protruded from his skin.

"I didn't hurt him," she whispered. "Please believe me. I did not do this."

"Then when my coroner gives me a time of death, you'll have an alibi." Larraby lifted a corner of the blanket with his pen. "I'm guessing sometime yesterday. So, Ella, care to change your story?"

Owen tightened his grip around her shoulders. "She wants to talk to a lawyer."

"Time to lawyer up? Not looking too innocent anymore are we?"

"I didn't kill him. I was abducted and spent the night in a ravine like I told you." Tears began to stream down Ella's face. "He is…was my friend." Owen held her tight, brain scrambling to find a way to fix it.

Larraby used the pen to pull the blanket farther away. "That's a farrier's rasp, isn't it?" he said, pointing to the metal shaft that protruded from Luke Baker's throat. "Yours? Your prints are on it? The other half of the one you gave me that was in your pocket?"

There was a sound of hushed voices and then Candy Silverton appeared around the corner of the carport. Her hair was swept into a neat platinum chignon, and a short man wearing a dark leather jacket followed one step behind. Bruce Reed, Owen figured.

Larraby held up a palm to stop her progress but Owen heard her sharp intake of breath as she saw the contents of the van. Her shriek cut through the air like bullet fire.

"Luke," she cried, trying to get to his body. "No, no it can't be." Her escort held her back.

"Candy," Reed said, face grave. "Don't look."

Candy's eyes went from the tool embedded in the flesh of her nephew's neck to Larraby and finally her gaze slid to Ella.

"You…you killed my nephew."

"I didn't," Ella said, voice hardly above a whisper. "I didn't. I… I think I was drugged, something in my thermos." She turned panicked eyes on Owen. "It dropped out of my van. If we can find it…"

Reed stared at Ella, eyes shifting in thought. Candy's mouth twisted. "Spare me the lies. You'll fry," she spat at Ella. "I'll see to it that you die for what you did to my nephew or I will kill you myself."

Ella turned her face to Owen's chest and clung to his shirt, barely able to stand.

"I didn't kill him…" she sobbed. "I didn't."

He caged her in a fierce embrace. "It's going to be okay," he said helplessly.

She pulled away, eyes bright with tears, shaking hands flat against his chest. "Owen, tell me you believe me."

He stared at her naked grief, the unadulterated terror. He saw in her face the little girl she had been, freckled, pesky, fun loving, now a woman, beautiful, desperate, vulnerable.

But there was the overwhelming evidence against her, her van, her farrier's rasp, the alcohol…

Trust was a dangerous thing, he knew, both from his work with horses and his time in the marines. It could blind you, cripple you, make you weak…but sometimes it could save your life.

He held her close, seeing his own reflection in

the tear-streaked green of her eyes. "Yes," he said. "I do believe you."

She cried harder then and looked in panic toward the house. "Please…"

He knew what she was asking. "I'll take care of Betsy and I'm gonna get you out of this."

Silverton was crying on Bruce Reed's shoulder, loud, gasping sobs. For a split second, Reed met Owen's eyes and he saw the sly, twisted gleam. *Evil*, he thought.

Owen glared full-on at the man and sent the message loud and clear. *You and I are enemies now.*

Larraby stepped forward, twisted Ella's hands behind her back and snapped on the handcuffs.

"You have the right to remain silent," he began.

In her cell, Ella squeezed herself into a ball. The shapeless tunic, pants and fabric slippers felt strange on her skin. Again, she started to check the time on her old trusty Timex and found it missing, taken by the police when she'd been booked.

The hours after the arrest and arraignment had blurred, and she could not quite believe it was her second day of incarceration. Every humiliating detail seemed like something from a nightmare; the strip search, the mug shot that left her dazed and finally the arraignment when she'd been marched into a crowded room and heard the charges against her.

Murder. The murder of Luke Baker, her friend.

An image of him bloodied and stuffed into her van surfaced before she could stop it, tears pricking her eyes. Then her memory shifted back to the moment when a court-appointed lawyer stood next to her as she made her plea.

Not guilty. She wanted to shout it, scream the words, stand in the chair and holler, "I am not a murderer. I am being framed," to anyone who would listen. But there were no friendly faces to appeal to, only people who saw her as a felon, guilty, going through the motions before she was tried and packed off to prison where she belonged.

And then the judge pronounced the bail at fifty thousand dollars. It might as well have been a million. There was no way she could come up with the required 10 percent to bond herself out of jail. Her bank account hovered just below two hundred dollars, since the doctor had changed Betsy's medicine to a more expensive variety that sucked up money faster than she could earn it.

Betsy. What was she thinking right now? She knew Owen would keep his word and find someone to take care of her, but her sister knew no other life except their quiet existence in Gold Bar. Who would cut up her toast into squares? Massage the muscles along her shoulders that tightened up? Turn on her favorite game show every night at seven thirty sharp? Who would pray with Betsy? All the things which had once seemed like chores were now precious connections that brought her closer to her sister than she'd ever thought possible.

Ella's throat constricted, but there were no more tears left. The other woman sharing her cell had not spoken a word, only turned her face to the wall and pulled the thin blanket up to cover her head.

"I don't belong here," she wanted to tell her cellmate. They'd taken a blood sample, but it might be too late to prove that she had not been drinking. Could it show that there was a drug in her system? If she could just find the thermos maybe there would be fingerprints on it.

The door clanged and she jumped. An officer stood there, beckoning. "Your bail's been posted."

"By whom?"

He lifted a shoulder. "Just come with me please, ma'am."

Her heart leapt. "So… I don't have to stay here?"

His eyebrows drew together. "You're out until you go to trial, or do something to violate your bail."

She heard the hardness in his tone. "Until they prove me guilty of murder, you mean?"

He shrugged, but she could tell that was exactly what he'd meant.

Enjoy the time before you're behind bars forever.

She padded after him and collected her meager belongings, though the police insisted on keeping her clothing and shoes. She was surprised to find a pair of worn jeans, her patched sweatshirt and her sneakers with the holes in them. Meekly, she pulled them on.

"Exit's that way, ma'am," the officer said, ushering her toward a door.

"But who posted my bail?"

"Guy named Owen Thorn," was the answer from the duty clerk.

Her stomach shrank into an aching knot. Humiliation complete, she was ushered through the exit door.

Owen saw her emerge, small and hunched as if she was expecting a blow. It twanged something inside him. He figured her release would be sometime that day so he'd camped out, waiting, asking his mom to go through Ella's house to find her some clean clothes, since he didn't feel it was right for him to go through her personal things. He rolled down the truck window, shoved back his cowboy hat with a thumb, and called to her.

She jerked, hesitating, and he thought she might ignore him, but then she walked over, head down, eyes on the ground.

"Let me give you a ride home."

She considered, still not looking at him.

"Come on," he prompted, getting out and opening the passenger door for her.

Finally she climbed in, hands twisted together in her lap.

He was not sure what to say. What were the right words after someone had been accused of murder and arrested? Words were not his strong suit at the best of times. "Betsy's okay," he said. "She's been staying at the ranch. Mom's happy to have her around. I think they're making pies today." Dumb, adding that pie thing, but he couldn't make his mouth say anything better.

Ella nodded.

"Uh, do you, er, need anything?"

"Could you give Betsy a ride home? I...they kept my van."

"No problem." He straightened, happy to have something concrete to do. "I'll drop you off and let you settle in while I go get her."

"Thank you, and thank you for posting my bond. I'll pay you back, every penny." The ferocity crept into her tone, and he was glad to hear it. Jail had not broken her spirit. *Stay angry,* he wanted to tell her. *Anger is a far better thing than despair.*

As the miles wound by she stared intensely out the window. She was searching, he realized.

"Stop, Owen, stop here. I think this is near the place where I got out of my van. If I can find my thermos, I can prove I was drugged."

He pulled to the side and prepared to get out with her. She turned tortured eyes on him. "Just drop me. I'll look and walk home. It's only a couple of miles. I don't need your help."

"Well, you're getting it anyway. I promised Ray…"

Her eyes rounded in horror. "You told him what happened?"

Now he'd done it. "He got wind of it somehow, maybe from his ex-wife. He called me and I could not lie to him."

"So now he knows I was arrested for murder and that the whole town thinks I killed Luke Baker in a drunken rage."

"No," Owen said firmly. "He thinks you were framed, just like I do, probably by Bruce Reed, and he's going crazy that he can't be here to help, but I told him I would get you out of this mess."

Her lips tightened in a grim line. "I don't need you to fix it. I will, and I'll show you all that I am telling the truth."

"I believe you."

"No, you don't. You just don't want Ray's little sister to be in prison."

"That's unfair."

"I don't care." Her mouth trembled, eyes feverish. "Nothing about this has been fair. I'm going to take care of myself and Betsy like I've always done. We don't need you and Ray to do anything." She got out and slammed the door.

He did the same, pulse ticking higher. If she was going to be a "firecracker," a word his twin Jack used for the most hot-blooded horses they worked with on the Gold Bar Ranch, then so be it. He wasn't about to turn away, no matter what she tossed at him.

"What are you doing?" she demanded.

He folded his arms and stared at her. "Protecting you from yourself. Now tell me where to start looking or I'll start a meter-by-meter perimeter search and we'll be here all day. Gonna get cold, you know. Forecast says we're in for a freeze, so the longer you dillydally…"

She glared at him, chin tipped to look up at him. Under any other circumstances he would have smiled.

"I'm not going to get rid of you, am I?"

"Not unless you think you can outwrestle me and I've got a hundred pounds and a foot and a half on you, so deal, Ella Jo."

She whirled away and he followed her, muttering something about him under her breath and peering into the piles of pine needles in a much less orderly fashion than he would have attempted.

"It's metal, painted green," she snapped, "with a twist-on top."

His head shot up as his senses detected the danger before his brain could react.

"Incoming," he shouted, grabbing her shoulder and shoving her to the side as a motorcycle hurtled off the road and straight for them.

FOUR

Ella could not process at first what was happening as the motorcycle bore down on them. Owen propelled her behind the nearest tree, which saved her from the impact of the churning tire. The driver's face was invisible behind the shaded visor of his helmet as he roared past, but his or her intent was clear. The motorcycle engine whined as he spun the bike into a 180-degree turn and came at them again.

By the time Ella scrambled to her feet, Owen had grabbed a fallen branch and planted himself in the path of the oncoming vehicle like a baseball player, ready to swing for the bleachers.

"Owen," she screamed. "What...?"

There was no time to finish the sentence as the motorcycle careened toward him. With a savagery in Owen's eyes she had never seen before, he swung the thick branch at the rider. The wood broke, ricocheting off the attacker's chest, shaking but not unseating him. The front wheel struck

Owen's leg and he grunted in pain, hitting the ground hard.

The motorcycle spun again and Ella could see that this time the driver meant not to miss his quarry. She dashed out, grabbed a rock and threw it as hard as she could at his helmet. Thanks to her days of pitching endless baseballs for Ray and Owen, her throw hit home with a crack as it struck the assailant's visor. It was not enough to stop him. Owen was trying to get to his feet, face tight with pain.

She found another rock and aimed to throw it when the sound of another vehicle cut the chilly air. She thought the motorcycle was going to come after them again regardless, but the driver wheeled away, disappearing down the road.

Jack Thorn leaped out of his truck and ran to his fallen brother. His blond hair and blue eyes marked them as twins, though not identical, his build more slender than Owen's, face narrower. He went to his knees next to Owen, gripping his arm.

"How bad?"

Owen breathed through his nose. "I'm okay," he grunted, teeth gritted.

Jack looked as though he did not believe his twin. His hand remained locked on his brother's arm, as if he could tell by the feel of the tensed muscles whether Owen was telling the truth or not.

Ella knelt next to them. "Whoever that was on

the motorcycle came after us. Owen tried to do some nutty Babe Ruth thing and knock him off the bike."

"Hank Aaron," Owen rasped, sucking in another breath, "not Babe Ruth, and I would have had him if the branch hadn't busted."

That seemed to be all the reassurance Jack needed. He leaned back on his heels, letting go of his brother but keeping a wary eye on him.

"Woman or man?" Jack asked.

Ella ripped her gaze from Owen. "What?"

"Was the driver a woman or a man?" Jack repeated patiently.

"A…" She wanted to say "man" but she had not seen enough to be sure. "I couldn't say for sure."

"Man," Owen said. "Too aggressive to be a woman."

Ella smiled at Owen's bit of ridiculous romanticism, or was it sexism? "I'm not going to dignify that statement with a comment." She shivered as the perspiration on her brow cooled in the winter temperatures. "Could have been either. Whoever it was must have been here first and didn't want me to find my thermos."

Owen waved away her offered hand and got to his feet, mouth tight, as Jack handed him his cowboy hat. "Bruce Reed. Has to be."

Her gut told her he was correct. "No way to prove it."

"We'll tell the cops," Jack said. "They can see

if Reed has a motorcycle registered to him. I'll call right now." He took out his phone and dialed.

Ella looked over the churned leaves and the mud rutted from their attacker's wheels. Nerves tightened in her stomach as she processed what had just happened. If Bruce Reed, or whoever that had been, was looking for the thermos, then she was right. It contained proof that she'd been abducted, proof that would force people to believe she was not a killer.

"It's here somewhere," she mumbled. "It has to be."

Owen began walking slowly through the detritus. She could tell he was trying hard not to limp, but his shoulders were still hunched with pain.

"You don't have to…" she started. His body tensed. Instinctively she knew it would wound him further just then to bring any more attention to his leg. A memory of Owen as a high school senior filled her mind, his anger at being sidelined during football season for a sprained ankle.

"I can play," he'd snapped at her. "Team relies on me."

"They can rely on someone else for a couple of games," she'd told him. She still remembered the look he'd given her then, eyes steely blue, glinting with passion.

"That's worse than the messed-up ankle."

Owen was a man who needed to be needed, a born protector. And what happened to the protec-

tor when he couldn't do the job anymore? She'd
never asked Owen about the severity of his injury,
but it had been a year since his return from Afghanistan and his limp was still detectable. Could
he expect a full recovery? She wondered what
would happen to Owen if the answer was no.

Forcing away the gloomy thought, she hurried
on with her search, allowing him some time to
collect himself, but she kept him in her peripheral
vision nonetheless.

If he required medical attention, she would see
to it that he got it whether he agreed or not.

After an irritating rehashing of the whole incident to Larraby and his promise to patrol the
area for the motorcycle, Owen endured the search,
though his leg felt like it was on fire. He purposely
kept back a few steps so Ella would not hear him
groan every time he bent over to probe a pile of
leaves. His body craved relief so badly he could
taste it.

There is no way around the pain, he told himself savagely. *No more pills, so get through it*. He
managed to scrape along for another hour until
Ella slapped a hand onto her thigh in frustration.

"It's just not here anywhere. It couldn't have
sprouted legs and wandered off by itself. The police didn't find it, so what could have happened
to it?"

"There's a river right down the slope past the trees. Could have rolled there and washed away."

She groaned.

"We have to call it a day. The temperature is dropping and we're losing the light. Mom just texted insisting I bring you to the ranch for some corn chowder."

She looked at her feet. "Um, I should just go home and…"

"Ella," he said firmly, waiting until she finally looked at him. "My family has known you since you were seven years old. They don't think for one minute that you're a killer."

Her cheeks went petal pink. "But they know, I mean, they heard that I did some drinking in the past. Maybe…"

"Maybe nothing. We were all different people four years ago. You made your peace with the Lord. You're forgiven."

She sighed. "I know that in my brain, but in my heart…"

He understood. Reaching out, he touched her cheek with his fingertip, her skin as satiny as a new leaf. "I get it. Hearts take a lot longer to learn than heads, don't they?"

She swallowed hard and he decided not to give her an opportunity to refuse, so he strode as best he could to the passenger-side door and opened it. She walked over. Just before she climbed in, she pressed a kiss to his cheek, startling him by the pleasure it sparked. Her lips were warm and soft, like the downy feathers of the new chicks his mom fussed over in the spring.

"I'm sorry, Owen. I'm sorry Bruce Reed hurt you, if that even was him."

Not as bad as I'm gonna hurt him for putting you through this. His thoughts surprised him. Not the protectiveness—he had always been ferociously protective of friends and family—but the tenderness that was twined around it.

Ray's sister, he reminded himself. *You owe it to him to take care of her. Period.*

Ray would never condone anything further between Owen and Ella. *Combat vets make lousy life partners*, was Ray's mantra. Ray was a good example, having endured a divorce after only two years of marriage. Owen still held out hope that Ray and Pam would reconcile one day, for the sake of them both and their daughter, Sarah, but Ray was an adrenaline junkie, never satisfied at home, always hankering for the next mission, too battle hardened to adjust to civilian life.

Owen felt the restlessness too, sometimes, the loss of his marine career and the pain of his injury had fueled his need for pills to dull the pain. The drugs had not healed his leg, nor had they assuaged the emptiness he felt from a military career cut short. He'd only shared some of these feelings with Jack and their church pastor, a former veteran himself, who'd counseled him when he'd hit the rock bottom of his life and fueled his determination to heal and reenlist.

At least he'd thought it was rock bottom. What if this was it? Trapped in a broken body, unable to rescue Ella from a life in prison? Imagining her in that harsh world, hurt him much more than the pain in his thigh.

Not gonna happen, Thorn, make sure of that. He made up his mind to return with a metal detector at first light and find the thermos if it took him all day.

The heater in the truck eased the muscle spasms in his leg and by the time they arrived at the Gold Bar Ranch, the agony had diminished. Ella hopped out of the truck before he could open the door for her and stopped a moment at the whitewashed fence to stroke Glory's silky muzzle. At fifteen hands high, the bay towered over her, lowering her head to accept the gentle caress.

"How's she doing?"

Owen was training Glory to be a cutting horse for ranch owner Macy Gregory's husband, Drake. "Good. She responds well to rein and leg pressure. Gaining some savvy with the steers and cows over at Macy's ranch." Macy's outfit was in neighboring Mountain Top where she kept a couple hundred head of cattle. It was more a hobby for the woman, as her real passion was competing in show jumping while her husband tended to the workings on their ranch. He'd heard Macy had curtailed her competing due to financial problems. "Haven't introduced Glory to any bulls yet." It was common misconception that horses and cows were naturally at ease around each other. It was possible to train any horse to work cows, but some horses just never got cow savvy. He had good hopes for the young filly.

"Pretty," Ella said.

Yes, Owen thought. Why had he never noticed how very pretty Ella was? The late sunlight tinted her hair with the rusty hues of fall. Her hands were delicate and strong as they traced over Glory's coat. More than pretty.

Shaking himself from his odd reverie, he led her into the house.

Ella went immediately to Betsy, who sat on a worn recliner, folding napkins on a tray table set in front of her. Ella kissed her and Owen left them to a moment of privacy. His mother was in the kitchen with his sister-in-law Shelby, looking at pieces of granite.

"For their new fireplace mantel," Shelby explained to him. His mother chuckled. "Betsy already pointed to her favorite. Want to weigh in?"

"All look like rocks to me," Owen said.

Shelby peered at the samples. "This one has more feldspar, which gives it a pinker hue."

"Leave it to an assayer to say something like that," his mother said with a smile.

Owen was glad to see his mother looking happier than she had in a very long time. Their grief at losing Bree, Barrett's first wife, would never completely disappear, but the whole ranch seemed somehow more cheerful now that Shelby had found a home there with his oldest brother.

He'd never worried much about finding a life partner when he was an active duty marine. He wasn't concerned about it in the slightest now either, because he intended to return to the marines as soon as humanly possible. So why was he suddenly hyperaware of Ella, sitting in the next room, laughing that belly laugh that had made him smile since she was a kid trailing after him?

"Owen?"

He realized his mother was looking at him. "Jack told me what happened. Are you sure you're okay?"

"Yeah. Hungry, is all."

"Hint taken," Shelby said, gathering up her granite samples. "I'll take these back to the cabin so we can get the table set."

His mother cocked her head, still looking at him. "How can we best help Ella?"

"I'm gonna figure that out."

"We," she repeated. "It's not all on you, Owen."

But as he caught sight of Ella holding her sister's hand, he did not agree. She was his childhood pal and his best friend's sister. The buck stopped with him. He would save Ella Cahill or die trying.

FIVE

Ella felt the elephant in the room in the way the Thorn family studiously avoided any mention of her current situation. Mrs. Thorn ladled out creamy bowls of corn chowder accompanied by hunks of corn bread.

Owen ate sparingly, she noticed, the lines of pain still prevalent on his forehead. Mr. Thorn chatted with his boys about the workings of their ranch and made sure to include Betsy in the conversation. Betsy beamed, nodding and even speaking a few words. Ella's heart swelled. It was good for her sister to be around a family. The Cahills hadn't exactly provided a ton of parental nurturing since their mother died when Ella was twelve. Their father, Shawn, was a hardworking, taciturn ex-military man who worked ridiculous hours as a long-distance trucker, relying on Ella and Ray to keep the household together and care for Betsy. The only time she'd ever seen him cry was at their mother's funeral, a trickle of tears down his weathered face, quickly wiped away.

After Ray's first deployment, the responsibility for Betsy's care had landed squarely on Ella's seventeen-year-old shoulders, and she had developed a full dose of resentment. At first she'd thought her brother would finish his service and come home to help her, but one deployment led to another, and then he'd married and started a new family. Though she'd never told him so, she'd resented him for having choices that seemed to be denied to her and Betsy.

And then when she was twenty two, Ray left for yet another overseas stint, then Owen left for his first deployment, and her father passed away. Ella had felt completely alone and mired in responsibilities that threatened to smother her. Thinking back on it, she relived the shame of how she'd acted out, gone to parties and started drinking, anything to escape what she felt was an impossible burden.

But waking up in the passenger seat of veterinarian Zeke Potter's van, the one she now owned, had been a wake-up call. She remembered the fear. *How long have I been away from Betsy? How long have I left her alone?* God both convicted her in that moment and changed her life.

Zeke had taken her home from the bus stop

where he'd found her passed out on his way back from tending the difficult birth of a calf.

"Ella Cahill, you're smarter than this," he'd said. "If you want to learn about animals, come see me."

And she had. He introduced her to a local farrier who taught her a trade, and she started reading her Bible again, taking Betsy to church with her whenever she could. She'd become such a good farrier, in fact, that she'd been solicited to work with the team that supported the US equestrian athletes in the Olympics. Oh, how she'd desperately wanted to accept, but there was no one to take care of Betsy, so she'd declined and walked away from her one and only chance. That hurt badly for awhile, but God had changed her feelings and her heart.

Yes, she'd given up the dreams she'd had for herself, but she was doing what she was meant to and the pain of deferred dreams had subsided to a soft, nostalgic ache.

The years passed in a blur, Owen and Ray re-enlisting and repeatedly redeploying. Ray coming home sporadically, and neither one ever bringing up her shameful behavior, though she was sure they both knew all about it. There were no secrets in small towns. How grateful she was that Jesus forgave, protected both her and Betsy on those wild and dangerous nights. The things that could have happened to her, to them both…

Stifling a shiver, she ate gratefully, the savory soup and bread almost warming the cold places inside her. But there was an axe hanging over her head, tethered by a very fine thread. At any moment she feared Larraby would plow through the door with some new evidence that would convict her without doubt.

Keegan, the youngest Thorn brother, sat back in his chair, wiping his mouth on the checkered napkin. "Okay, so I'm just gonna say it. I mean, I know we aren't supposed to talk about your troubles, Ella, but I've seen someone out riding the trails at night on a motorcycle."

Everyone fell silent, staring at him.

He shrugged. "I like bikes, so I pay attention to stuff like that. Jack told me he had seen the same thing when he was flying around in the Death Trap."

"Death Trap?" Ella asked.

Owen shook his head. "His ultralight aircraft."

"Basically a toaster with wings," Keegan said. "Anyway, there's a biker using the trails around here."

Owen put down his spoon. "Who's the rider? Same guy who tried to take us out?"

"Dunno, but I was thinking maybe we can find out. That would help, right?" He eyed his brother with a sly smile. "The front fender probably has a little dent from Owen's knee in it."

Owen didn't smile back but Ella could see the amusement in his eyes. "A big dent."

Keegan laughed. "I stand corrected. I figured Jack and I can check out the ridgeline where I saw the guy riding. Follow the trail if there is one back to finding out where he came from. How 'bout it, Jack?"

Jack nodded, pushing his plate away.

"I'll go too," Owen said.

"No."

Ella had not heard Jack argue with his brother before. His quiet voice was firm. "You take Ella and Betsy home." Ella had already made it clear they had no plans of staying on the Thorn ranch in spite of Evie Thorn's offer.

Owen locked eyes with Jack.

"Take care of Ella. She should be your priority." Jack's tone was light enough, but something in the downward turn of his mouth hinted of pain. Jack was probably thinking of Shannon Livingston, Ella's best friend and the love of his life. She'd walked out on Jack to go to medical school, taking his heart with her.

Barrett cleared his throat. "He's right, Owen. Best to get Ella and Betsy settled in."

Owen hesitated for another moment before he tossed his napkin on the table. "Okay. I'm gonna find that thermos tomorrow and pay Bruce Reed a visit."

Ella gasped. "No, Owen. He's dangerous."

His mouth hardened into a grim line and the look in his eyes scared her. "So am I," he said.

Owen downed a couple of aspirin when no one was looking. It dulled the throbbing, if only temporarily, before he led Ella and Betsy to the big ranch van they'd gotten when Grandad became wheelchair bound. It was roomier than his truck, for sure, with a lift to ease Betsy into position with more comfort than him moving her.

They were back at her little house by seven, as the last glimmers of sunlight faded to black. He noticed afresh how the structure was shrouded by a thick border of trees, set back from the road. Isolated.

He jerked toward a faraway buzz of engine noise as he lowered Betsy's wheelchair from the truck. Not a motorcycle, just a horse trailer rumbling away from Candy Silverton's ranch.

You'll fry.

Her words rang in his memory, but even louder was the clear message written on Bruce Reed's face, a bold statement that he was a man who would get whatever he wanted and eliminate whoever was in his way. Owen suspected what Bruce wanted was Candy's millions. He watched Ella open the front door and usher her sister into the house.

"Ella," he called to her. "Okay if I do a quick check of your windows and doors?"

"I…" She had started to protest. "I guess that's a good idea."

Of course it was a good idea, but it would take some getting used to. No one in the town of Gold Bar, the Thorns included, ever locked anything. They hadn't needed to, until now.

When he'd returned to the Gold Bar after his first deployment, he'd fought the urge to secure the ranch tight. Naive boy no longer, he knew there was evil and death because he'd seen it, escaped it, mourned for those who hadn't. But he would not allow those feelings to color his actions at home because he did not want Gold Bar, nor his perception of it, to change.

But it had anyway. He remembered the night after his second deployment when he'd grabbed a rifle and gone to check on a noise, only to scare his mother half to death as she warmed tea.

The look on her face, the mug shattering on the floor, his grip on the rifle.

"Owen," she'd breathed. "Owen, is that…you?"

He realized later that his face, his demeanor, must have been so hardened into a mask of hatred, that he'd likely scared her half to death. He'd promptly re-upped and then he was back in Afghanistan, the only place where things made sense. He'd come a long way since then, understood his desire to be alone, and the need to share with people who could help him.

You're better. His mind, maybe, but his body

still scoffed at him, the leg twinging in mockery. He would overcome that too. He mentally chided himself for not making the next physical therapy appointment. Perhaps it was fear that kept him from going, rather than procrastination. What if his doctor said there was no chance he could resume his military career? What then?

He walked the outside perimeter of the house too, checking that the screens were in place and exterior doors were locked. Then he examined the inside, trying not to show Ella that he noticed the locks were cheap and many of them were rusted. One window would simply not lock properly for all his forcing, so he cut part of a broomstick and wedged it in the track.

Ella played the messages back on her answering machine connected to the house phone. He marveled at the old avocado green device with the curly cord. But that was Gold Bar for you—a town with a foot in the present and the other firmly planted in the past.

Though he tried not to listen, it was impossible to miss her body language. With each message, her shoulders sank lower.

"...*Went with another farrier.*"

"...*No longer require your services.*"

"...*Got someone else to do the work.*"

Ella's lips trembled and she did not look at him. "They all think I'm guilty. No one wants a murderer working for them."

He laid hands on her shoulders and massaged gently. "It's only temporary. We're gonna clear this all up." Her shuddering breaths told him she was trying hard not to cry so he turned her around and held her in his arms, tucking her head under his chin.

"I've worked so hard," she whispered. "Every night for months to complete farrier school. I put every penny I saved into starting my business."

He tightened his hold. "Ella, I'm going to fix this. I promise."

The house phone rang and after a moment of hesitation, Ella stepped out of his embrace and answered. Whatever she heard made her jerk so violently, she let go of the phone, sending it dangling toward the floor. He snatched it up and put it to his ear.

Candy Silverton's voice was almost unrecognizable, twisted with rage. "You didn't have to kill him. I would have loaned you money. You selfish, no good piece of trash."

"Ella didn't kill your nephew," he said over her wailing. "So knock it off."

"Oh yes she did, and I'm going to make sure she pays with her life."

The line went dead.

He replaced the phone on the cradle. Ella folded her arms tight across her chest. "She has a lot of influence in this town. I'm sure she's told everyone that I killed Luke."

He answered when his phone vibrated. His brother Keegan spouted the info so quickly he could barely catch it all. When he disconnected, he lifted Ella's chin until she looked at him.

"We just got a break. My brothers found the motorcycle hidden in a gorge and gave the license plate number to Larraby. Keegan has a girl he once dated who works for a private eye. He asked her to run the plates. Guess who it's registered to?"

"Who?"

"Bruce Reed. Jack phoned the cops and Larraby's away at the moment but he'll head over to talk to Reed first thing Monday."

A streak of hope broke across her face. "So we might be able to prove he tried to run us down, but how will that get me off the hook for murder?"

"I dunno," he said, grabbing his jacket. "But it's got to help us show Bruce Reed for what he really is."

"You can't go over there Monday, Owen, if that's what you're thinking."

"Sure I can. It's a free country and I'd like to hear Candy Silverton explain to Larraby that she just called and threatened your life."

"Everyone will be angry at your intrusion," she said. "Larraby, Candy Silverton, Bruce Reed…"

"You know," he said, smiling at her, "I just don't really care."

"Don't get in trouble for me."

"Ella, I've risked my life for people I will never meet. You, I've known since you were in grade school." As he looked at those lush green eyes, his heart started beating to a faster tempo, the pulse thundering loud in his ears. He cleared his throat. "You're my best friend's sister and my family loves you. Why wouldn't I take a risk for you?"

"Because I don't want you to," she said firmly. "Because this isn't your battle."

"Well, I'm making it my battle."

"Why?"

"I just told you."

"No. You could let the police handle it. Family friendship doesn't go this far. Ray would understand."

"No, he wouldn't."

She blew out a breath that ruffled her bangs. "You've nearly been run down. Isn't that enough?"

He fought to keep his tone level. "Have we cleared your name yet? Have we gotten back everything you've lost? Your work? Your reputation? Your freedom?"

"No," she said, voice breaking.

"Then I guess you have your answer."

SIX

Ella paced the small front room in the wee hours of Monday morning. She was unsettled at having missed church service the day before, but she could not bring herself to walk into the tiny church and face the curious and suspicious glances. Instead she read a Bible passage to Betsy, sang some songs and watched a television worship service on their fuzzy old TV.

It had brought no relief. Nor had the fruitless search for her thermos. She could not rid her body of the oppressive worry, no matter how much she prayed. Compounding her fears was the knowledge that Owen was likely going to go all Rambo and interfere with Larraby's investigation. It was one thing to watch her own life implode, but she could not stand by and watch Owen do the same while he was acting like some macho cowboy marine. Cowboy pride was bad enough, but mix that with a stubborn military streak and it had disaster written all over it. She knew firsthand.

Her father Shawn was as stubborn as they came, and her brother, Ray, only a hair less. She'd seen them both standing outside in the freezing rain for hours to complete a target shooting contest because neither one could admit defeat.

Before sunup, she'd decided on a plan of action. She'd swallowed her pride, phoned Shelby and begged a favor. It pained her to think that the Thorn family members were probably some of the few people in town on whom she could rely. Owen, she learned from Shelby, was out working a horse and intended to ride it to Silverton's ranch later that morning in time for Larraby's visit, which he had somehow discerned was at ten o'clock. Shelby agreed to come over and stay with Betsy until she departed for the airport with Barrett to visit Shelby's mother. Ella did not tell Shelby she was bent on intercepting Owen before he interfered. She'd have to start the walk to Silverton's ranch soon since she had no vehicle.

By the time the doorbell rang Ella had received three additional farrier job cancellations. Her spirit nosedived with each one. Stomach in knots, she was about to open the door when she remembered the hatred in Candy's voice. Peeking through the window, she was surprised to find the town veterinarian Zeke Potter standing on the porch.

She threw it open, breath held. Would she see suspicion in her mentor's eyes? Fear? It would be the final knife in her heart.

Instead he held his beefy arms wide and she tumbled in.

"I didn't do it," she babbled. "I didn't."

"Awww, I know," he said, squeezing her against his round stomach. When he let her go, she noticed his eyes were bloodshot, the scruff of beard showing on his unshaven face. "I been telling anyone who will listen that it wasn't you."

"Thank you," she said with a hard swallow. "It means the world that you believe me."

"'Course I do. And so do others, plenty of them." He shook his head until his second chin jiggled. "Terrible thing. Luke was not much of a hard worker, but he was an okay kid. Think he got mixed up in something? Gambling, maybe? That's a dirty business. No forgiveness there."

Ella lowered her voice so Betsy would not hear. "I think Bruce Reed might be involved."

Zeke's eyes widened. "Nah, why would he do that? Kill the nephew of the gal he's moving in on?"

"Luke suspected Reed of crimes, I don't know what in particular."

Zeke shook his shaggy head. "This is all too much for this old guy. I'm not going to bother about Reed and neither should you. You're out of jail, right? They must not think you're too dangerous." He cracked a grin that revealed a chipped front tooth, lost to a kick from an irate goat, she knew.

"I'm out on bail. It's temporary," she forced herself to say.

"Well, how do we go about making it permanent?"

"First thing is I need to find my thermos." She explained about the kidnapping. "If I can prove I was drugged, that would go a long way. There might even be fingerprints."

He nodded thoughtfully. "Okay. I'll see if I can look for it. Ask around. Maybe somebody picked it up from the side of the road. In the meantime, I thought you could use my pickup. Heard the cops are holding your van. I got the big truck, so you can borrow the pickup until you get your wheels back."

Her eyes filled. "How can I ever thank you, Zeke?"

He waved a calloused hand. "Ah, no need to get all mushy. I ain't all that much of a prize."

Still, he accepted her grateful hug. "Shelby Thorn is coming to stay with Betsy. Can we get the truck as soon as she arrives?"

"Sure, sure." His phone rang. "Gonna take this. Candy Silverton's just put a deposit on six broodmares and she's nervous as a cat. Gotta check them out for her."

Ella remembered a snippet of conversation she'd had with Luke.

Bruce is pushing her to buy horses to breed.

He's handling the purchase. Says they're worth a bundle and the paperwork backs him up.

But you don't think so? Ella had asked.

Time will tell, I guess.

But there hadn't been enough time, not for Luke. She blinked away the memory of finding his body in the back of her van with her very own farrier's rasp buried in his neck. The audacity of the crime floored her. The killer had drugged her tea and planted Luke's body in her van. Bile rose in her throat.

Priority number one was to hustle to Candy Silverton's ranch and prevent Owen Thorn from getting into trouble on her account. If she had a chance while she was there to lay eyes on the broodmares, she wouldn't mind that either. She wasn't an expert on breeding stock by any means, but she could certainly tell a healthy equine specimen when she saw one.

If Candy Silverton was too misled by Bruce Reed to see the truth…

Zeke hung up the phone. "Gonna take a gander at them later today."

"Be careful," she blurted.

He cocked his head. "Nothing's gonna happen to an ancient country vet."

"Bruce Reed is dangerous. If you cross him, he'll hurt you."

Zeke went silent for a moment. "This will all work out, Ella, you'll see."

She wished she could believe it too.

Owen's leg was telling him he should not still be riding Glory after their early morning session, but he wanted the horse to get the feeling of the trail he took them on, which turned into more of a cut through at some places than a regular path. It was one thing to take a horse along well-manicured trails, but the more rough and tumble the conditions, the better she would perform later. The thousand acres of Gold Bar Ranch offered a bounty of opportunities for an eager, or not so eager, new horse.

It reminded him of the new "boots," the soldiers who arrived for their first deployment with a slightly glazed look as they struggled to take in the reality of living in a war zone half a world away from their hometowns. There was no cure for that disorientation but to accept it, change your own expectations and become someone else. The trouble was, when you got home, everyone expected you to be the same person who'd deployed. It was not fair. It was not even possible.

Owen felt again the sensation that he did not belong anymore in Gold Bar, or anywhere else. As much as he desperately wanted to be the same Owen Thorn, he wasn't, and he would never be.

Could he accept it? He offered up a prayer. *Help me find my way again, Lord.*

With effort, he pulled himself back to the moment as Glory took the final sloping path that overlooked Candy Silverton's property. Larraby's police car was already parked at the bottom of the drive. He was surprised to find Zeke Potter's old pickup idling at the gated end of the long sweeping entrance to the property and even more surprised to find Ella sitting behind the wheel. She cut the engine and got out.

"You're not going down there," she said.

He straightened in the saddle, biting back the urge to retort. After a breath, he slid off the horse and faced her.

"Told you I'm gonna hear what Reed has to say."

"You're going to make things worse."

"I don't see it that way."

"Well, news flash, you're not the boss here, Owen."

"Someone has to be," he snapped. "You're out on bail, Ella. You're on borrowed time." He regretted his words immediately. Her lips quivered, just for a moment, long enough for him to realize he'd made her feel small and helpless.

"I'm sorry," he said. "That was unkind. I'm... I default to commander when I don't know how to react. It's just the only way I know sometimes."

She held out her hand and he took it, small

and warm against his calloused palm. The earnest shine on her face made his breath catch.

"I understand you're trying to help me and I appreciate it." She quirked a smile. "Besides, it's really not that out of character for you. You were always a bossypants, just like Ray."

He laughed. "Nobody's bossier than Ray."

"You'd like to think so. But having two bossy men taught me I had to be smarter and quicker than both of you."

He flashed on a memory of her—freckles and pigtails flying, perched on the top of the rock she'd just scaled. *Catch me if you can, Owen!*

He felt lighter, easier, all of a sudden. That was like Ella, he thought, to make a man's shortcomings easier to bear. Strong and tender at the same time. He squeezed her hand, reluctant to let it go, but he did anyway.

In the distance they watched a stableboy load six horses into a trailer.

"Guy's not very good at it—he's forcing them too much," Owen said.

"That's Tony. Candy hired him a few months ago, but I don't recognize the horses." She moved to the split rail fence and looked closer. "Those must be the mares Bruce Reed is pressuring Candy into buying. Zeke's supposed to examine them later today, so why is Tony loading them, I wonder?"

"I'll see if I can find out while I'm down there.

Hang on to Glory for me," he said, pushing the reins at her.

"Too late." She pointed to the end of the drive where Larraby was getting into his car and leaving.

Owen muttered under his breath. "He was early."

In a few moments, Larraby drew level with them.

"What are you two doing here?"

"What did Reed say about the motorcycle?" Owen fired back.

"How did you know about that?"

Owen lifted a shoulder. "Friends in high places."

"Stay out of this investigation, Owen."

"Tell me what he said."

Larraby considered, mouth in a tight line. "I guess it won't hurt for you to know that Reed claims his motorcycle was stolen two days ago."

Owen rolled his eyes. "Of course he does."

"Nothing to prove him a liar."

"Did you talk to Candy about her phone threats?" Ella said.

"Yeah. Says she was overcome, promises it won't happen again."

Owen grunted. "And you believe her?"

"Reed assured her that Ella was going to prison, so she's content with that for now."

Ella blanched and Owen put a protective hand

on the small of her back. "We're not going to let that happen."

"Both of you get out of here." Larraby gunned the motor and drove away.

Owen climbed into the saddle.

Ella gave him a quizzical look. "Where are you going?"

"Gonna ride to the top of the ridge to see where that horse trailer is headed."

"Do you think it has something to do with Reed's scheming?"

"That guy's slipperier than an eel. If his fingers are in that horse purchase, it's shady for sure."

"I'll follow in the truck."

He winked at her. "Catch me if you can."

SEVEN

She was able to shadow Owen and Glory fairly closely, finally parking the truck and hiking up a steep grassy incline to meet him. Glory was tethered to a tree, cropping grass.

Owen was on his belly, peering through binoculars down into the valley below. "Good restraint, lead foot. I figured you might beat me here."

"I might have, since you ride at turtle speed."

He chuckled, not taking his eyes off the binoculars.

His position made her smile. They'd played cops and robbers during many hot sultry days, and they'd used every suitable rock pile as a lookout. As she looked closer at the hardness of his jaw, the steely set to his mouth, she became aware that it was no longer a game for Owen. The things he had seen, done…they'd changed him. There was very little of the playful, outgoing boy about him. Then again, hadn't her own struggles changed her too?

No condemnation, she reminded herself when the burden became too heavy. Forgiven, God said so, but forgiven didn't mean forgotten by human standards. Plenty of people were probably remembering her past bad choices in light of her current trouble. She shrugged off the thoughts.

"He's stopped just down the hill," Owen said, breaking into her thoughts. "He got out and moved west about twelve meters. Probably trying to find cell reception. I'm going closer to get a look at those horses." He climbed awkwardly to his feet.

This time she didn't try to talk any sense into him; she just fell in behind.

"Want to wait here with Glory?" he tried, blue eyes set off by the vast cloudless sky behind him.

"No, thanks."

He grumbled something under his breath. "I figured."

"Catch me if you can," she said as she walked by him down the slope.

He kept close behind her. The hill was peppered with oaks set tightly together, the still-brown grass waving in clumps higher than their shins in the winter wind. Tony had driven down the seldom-used road and then parked the thirty-six-foot trailer pulled by a truck under cover of a screen of trees. *Why?* she wondered. The winding road was not the fastest way to get out of town, and probably not the safest, with such a large vehicle, even a top-of-the-line rig like this one.

"Looks like a hotel on wheels," Owen muttered. "The trailer alone probably costs more than all of our vehicles combined."

"Candy bought it recently, in the past three months, from a friend of Reed's. He went with her to pick it up, I remember."

"Of course he did."

She stepped over a pile of rocks. "He certainly doesn't seem to mind spending her money."

They grew quiet as they neared the road, moving slowly.

"He's yakking on the phone, looks like," Owen whispered. He spoke into her ear, his mouth tickling her cheek, prickling her skin in goose bumps.

"I'm going to see if I can peek in the trailer window," she whispered.

"We'll go together because you're not tall enough to see in without a boost."

She jabbed him with her elbow. "Funny."

As they drew closer, there was no sign of Tony. They crept around the side of the rig and Ella poked her head up, annoyed to find that Owen was right. She was not tall enough to get a good look. Owen stood back a pace, grinning.

Ignoring him, she crept to the wheel hub to give herself a boost just as Tony appeared around the passenger side. She froze.

He had a rifle leveled at her head.

* * *

Owen raised his hands and shuffled slowly toward Tony, hoping to get between Ella and the rifle.

"Take it easy, fella," he said. "Saw your trailer here. Need some help?"

Tony glared. "Nice try. If you move one inch closer, I'll shoot you."

The comment angered Owen. Heat crawled up his throat. "I've been shot at by way more skilled gunmen than you. You even know how to use that thing?"

Tony shot off a round that whistled between him and Ella, burying itself into the wood of a gnarled oak.

From inside the trailer came a series of anxious whinnies.

Now Owen was properly furious, but he tried to keep a lid on his boiling temper. "Upsetting Miss Silverton's new horses? You're gonna get fired for sure."

"Shut up, Owen. I heard about you. Think you're some kind of hero? Like you own this town or something because you served? Big deal. You're gonna look the same dead as all your Marine brothers."

Owen went still, his muscles filled with the urge to strike out. "Don't speak about my guys, punk. Every one of them is twice the man you'll ever be."

Tony looked from Ella to Owen, his deep-set eyes sizing them up. "Pretty bold words for a guy who's trying to mess with Miss Silverton's property."

"We weren't doing anything of the kind," Ella snapped. Owen noticed Tony's grip tighten on the gun.

"You snuck up on my trailer and I'm just defending myself," Tony said. "You're in the wrong."

"What are you doing out here?" Ella said. "Where are you taking these horses?"

"None of your business." He cocked his head. "Thought you were in prison."

Owen started to answer, but she cut him off. "I'm not guilty and I'm going to prove it." She moved again to step up on the wheel hub.

Tony aimed the gun at her head. "Get down."

Owen tensed, calculating the distance between him and Tony. Too far to take him out before he got a shot off. It would be so satisfying to bring him down and teach him some respect, but he could not risk Ella getting shot.

She stared at Tony. "Why don't you want us to see these horses? Who told you to take them away? Bruce Reed? Why doesn't he want Candy to get a good look at them?"

"None of your business. Now get out of here, both of you, before I start shooting." He grinned. "Or better yet, I can call the cops. Don't think you're wanting any more trouble than you've already got, isn't that right?"

Owen stepped forward, desiring nothing more than to erase the smug smile on Tony's face. Ella caught the back of his shirt.

"He's right, Owen. Let's go."

Owen didn't budge. "Not moving until he backs off with that rifle. I think he can't hit the broad side of a barn and he's only gonna get a chance for one shot, so it better be center mass."

She tugged harder as a look of fear crept across Tony's face. He eased up on the gun. "I'm driving out of here but if either one of you so much as touches this trailer, I'll shoot."

Pulse hammering, teeth ground together, Owen watched Tony get behind the wheel and start the trailer moving slowly up the slope.

Owen realized he was trembling with rage, his breath coming in angry bursts as he paced away a few steps, trying to conceal his lack of control.

Then she was behind him, lassoing him in a loose hug, and he relaxed a bit into the blissful sensation.

"It's okay," she said quietly.

"Not okay when a guy like that points a gun at you. He's got no right."

She rubbed circles of comfort into his taut muscles. "It must be hard to endure." She paused a minute. "So different than your experiences in Afghanistan. Ray's said so too."

He felt the swirl of disconnection so strong at that moment. Two worlds, two lives. "Yeah. Over there, when someone points a gun at me, I know what to do, it's instinct and training, so clear, but then I gotta remind myself this isn't war." He heaved out a breath. "I don't know how to be at peace. I was made for war, Ella." His own words surprised him and the swirl of sadness that accompanied them.

She gently turned his shoulders so he was facing her. "You were made for other things too." Her smile was so sweet and tender that his throat clogged for a moment.

"Did you get help?" she asked. "I mean, I heard that things were tough after you came home with the injury and the adjustment to being stateside and all."

"Yeah. The injury was a bear. Couldn't get off the pain pills by myself." He looked deep into her eyes, fearing what he would see there, but the green depths remained unclouded with judgment, disappointment or even surprise. She must have known, must have heard, about his addiction. *Small town*, he thought ruefully. "It's my body that's not getting the message." He looked down. "Leg is slow to heal right. Damage is deep. As far as adjusting to civilian life…" He shrugged. "Guess I haven't, not fully."

She reached up and stroked his cheek. The tension drained from him and left behind a quiet longing, a desperate need to stay right there in the comfort of her embrace, as if that square foot of ground they stood on was the only place he really did belong.

"I'll keep praying for you," she said.

She would pray for him? A woman facing prison and death threats? Pray for a guy who left her alone just like her brother to fend for herself? He was overcome and for a moment he could not find words. She raised up on tiptoe, cupped his face and pressed her lips gentle as a whisper to the corner of his mouth.

He stood frozen, completely paralyzed and befuddled by his own emotions until she moved away. His heart pounded a solemn reminder. *Ray's sister. Ray's kid sister.* But in that moment she looked like anything but a kid.

"I'd better go," she said. "I need to get back to Betsy."

He cleared his throat. "Right. Gotta get Glory home and tend to her. Then I'm going to find your thermos and figure out how to dig up some intel on Bruce Reed."

Mission firmly in place, he followed her back through the tall grasses with only the barest lingering warmth on his mouth left by her kiss.

Ella's head was still spinning as she returned from a fruitless search for her thermos. She'd scoured the shoulder of the road for as long as she could, stopping home every few hours to check on Betsy. Her cheeks went hot every time someone drove by, no doubt staring at the jailbird plowing through the fallen leaves.

Her hands were scratched, bones chilled by the winter temperatures. She was grateful to find that Peg and Mary from the Sunrise Café had delivered some clam chowder and a crusty loaf of sourdough in her absence, after visiting a bit with Betsy. She was pleased she had given them a key to her place. Her heart swelled to know that she still had a few friends in Gold Bar.

Praying for you, their note said. She'd take all the prayers she could get.

She watched a few minutes of *Jeopardy!* with Betsy and set to work reheating the soup, the fragrance making her mouth water.

Betsy giggled at something she heard on the TV and Ella felt a pang. What would happen to Betsy if Ella went to prison? Her sister was born with an AVM, arteriovenous malformation, a tangle of blood vessels in her brain that ruptured and caused a stroke. Doctors saved her life but the damage was done: partial paralysis, aphasia, vision loss, loss of understanding. What scared Ella even more was that it could happen again.

She realized she was holding the ceramic bowls in a death grip. Forcing her fingers to relax, she brought the meal to the little tray table, earning a smile from her sister. As they watched and ate, she wondered how to prepare Betsy for the possible worst-case scenario. What should she say to her sweet, trusting sister to explain why her little sis, her best friend, her caretaker, might wind up spending the rest of her life in jail?

She was still trying to wrestle with the idea when she heard a soft mewling. She turned the TV down. "Did you hear that?"

Betsy nodded.

There had been a pregnant tabby cat prowling her yard earlier. She had hoped it had gone somewhere else to have babies, but the space underneath the wheelchair ramp seemed to be just cozy enough to attract all manner of critters. The last thing she needed was a litter of kittens to worry about.

With a sigh, she put the soup aside, turned the TV back up and looked out the front window. The yard was dark, lit only by a sliver of moonlight. She turned on the porch light. There was no sign of a kitty, or any other signs of life, but the plaintive mewing remained.

With a sigh she grabbed a flashlight and opened the door. Closing it behind her to keep in the expensive heat, she walked to the end of the ramp, shining the flashlight underneath.

A gloved hand fastened on her wrist. She screamed, dropping the flashlight, but the grip on her wrist held like an iron band and she was imprisoned, looking into the face of Bruce Reed.

EIGHT

"Let go," Ella hissed.

"Not until we come to an understanding," Reed said. His eyes were black slits in the glare of the porch light, teeth eerily white.

"Did you play the kitten sounds to lure me outside?"

"I wanted to talk. I knew you wouldn't open the door."

She tried to yank her wrist away, but he twisted her arm, marching her backward until she smacked into the railing. "You remind me of my ex-wife. So small and so stubborn."

Ella pitied whomever Bruce Reed had conned into marrying him. She sucked in a breath to scream.

He laughed. "Go ahead. No one out here to notice."

"Betsy will call the police." Ella had taught her how to dial 9-1-1 on their phone.

"Oh, then in that case you'd better not scream,"

he said with a smile. "Or I might have to go in there and persuade her not to."

Her breath caught. "Don't. I won't scream."

"Okay, then." He kept her wrist with one hand in a grip that never lessened. With the other, he traced a finger along the collar of her jacket. She recoiled.

If she could aim a kick, an elbow…but her body was numb with fear. She knew without question that Bruce Reed was the one who had drugged her, positioned her behind the wheel of her van, the killer who had ended Luke Baker's life and tried to frame her for it. If she had any doubts at all, they vanished as she looked into his cold eyes.

She had to play for time, until she could force her body to overcome the fear. "Why did you kill him?"

"That's not what we are going to talk about, Ella. These accusations about me you're spreading with the help of your boyfriend, they won't do."

She stayed quiet.

"Accusations that I drugged you…" His tone was casual but there was steel underneath. "So silly, all this talk from an accused killer. Just makes you look desperate."

"I'm going to prove you did it."

"No," he said, shoving her harder against the railing, his hands going around her throat. "You are going to keep your mouth shut and if you don't, you will die."

She tried to pry away his fingers as he cut off her oxygen.

"I'm not going to kill you now, you understand," he said, squeezing. "This is just a message, a warning, because I believe every nag should have a chance to run, you know?" His face was close to hers. "I'm poised for the score of a lifetime, and no scrawny little low-class girl is going to mess things up for me."

She shot out a knee, but he deflected it. She tried to answer, but only a gargling croak came from her throat.

"I am telling you to keep your mouth shut and stop spreading manure about me. Maybe you'll get out of the murder rap, or maybe you won't, but if you make more trouble for me, I will kill you." With each word he tightened his grip on her throat.

She felt herself starting to go limp. Desperately she tried to wriggle free.

He put his mouth to her ear and held his lips along the side of her face. "I love the ones that fight back," he whispered.

She fought against the closing darkness, trying to scratch at his hands, his face, but terror and oxygen depletion robbed her of strength.

Help me.

"And if you go to the cops, guess what will happen to your sister?"

Specks of light danced in front of her eyes. *Betsy. Not Betsy.*

"So vulnerable, isn't she?" he breathed. "Trapped in that chair. Confused, so trusting, like a little newborn foal. It wouldn't be hard, not hard at all. It would look like a tragic accident. I can make anything look like an accident."

With shaking hands she raised up a finger to gouge at his eye but her muscles trembled so much she couldn't manage it.

She collapsed to her knees. Her clouded senses picked up a familiar sound, but her brain was too addled to decipher it.

"You know," he said, "maybe I'll just take care of that part now. Sounds like *Jeopardy!* is almost over. I'll just go inside and pay Betsy a visit."

"No," she rasped. "No, no."

He laughed, slid his hands to her shoulders, bent close and pressed a kiss to her temple. Bile filled her, disgust so thick it was almost smothering.

Then he was moving away, toward the door, toward Betsy.

Panic enabled her to get to her knees. *Crawl if you have to. Get a knife, the baseball bat in the hall closet, anything.* But her limbs were shaking so bad, she sprawled to the ground.

Get up, she silently screamed. *Save your sister.*

Tires echoed along the road leading to her cabin. A neighbor coming to check on her?

The sound of a car door flung open.

Running feet.

The scream remained locked in her swollen throat.

Forcing herself onto all fours, she crawled two painful steps.

The front door lock clicked into place. Reed was inside with her sister.

Owen ran. He saw just enough glint of moonlight to see Ella pulling herself up from the ground. *I never should have left her here unprotected.*

Nerves exploded as he skidded to a stop next to her.

"Ella…"

She grabbed his arm with such force her nails dug into his skin.

"Betsy," she rasped. "He's inside with my sister."

He? Bruce Reed? Owen ran to the truck, grabbed his rifle and pounded to the front door. It was locked. He hammered as hard as he could.

"Open up, Reed. Right now."

There was no sound from inside. Options. Police would take too long. He could break a window, but that would take time and Betsy might catch flying glass if she was near. The door was a simple bolt lock kind. He would have kicked it in before his injury.

Not the marine you used to be.

Shoving that thought away, he set aside the gun and rammed his shoulder into the wood, just above the doorknob. The panel shuddered, enough to let him know it would give way eventually.

Again and again he hit the door with the full weight of his body. Bits of wood splintered off and he knew it was weakening. But the moments were precious with Reed inside. Two more vicious rams with his throbbing shoulder and the door gave, the lock shearing off with a shrill creak. He kicked it open, grabbed his rifle and charged through.

"Reed," he bellowed. "I'm coming for you."

Silence, except for a whimper.

He crawled to the end of the pony wall, ducked low, counted to three and hurtled around the partition, gun aimed.

Betsy screamed.

He pulled up, scanning the room.

"Betsy, where's the man?"

She pointed a shaking finger toward the back sliding door, which was open, the breeze blowing the curtains aside.

"He left?" Owen said.

She nodded, eyes wide with fear.

He ran to the open door in time to see taillights vanishing into the darkness.

When he returned, Ella was inside, kneeling next to Betsy, sobbing on her sister's lap.

He left the gun accessible, but far enough away

that it wouldn't scare Betsy unnecessarily. When Ella lifted her head at his approach, his heart seized up. Red welts stood out on her throat, finger marks where Reed must have tried to strangle her.

He went hot all over as he helped her up, easing her onto the chair next to her sister. As far as he could tell, Betsy appeared unharmed, but fear had robbed her face of any color. "It's okay, Betsy," he whispered. "Your sister is hurt. I'm just going to take care of her for a minute, okay?"

Betsy nodded, still clutching Ella's hand.

Ella sat, sucking in air, coughing, struggling for breath. He knelt next to her, pushed her hair back, grazing fingers over her bruised skin. Her pulse hammered a frantic beat under her touch.

Rage, hot and caustic, bubbled through him, but now was not the time to let it run free. "I'm calling an ambulance, the cops," he managed.

Now she came to life, clutching his shirt, holding him in place. "No."

It was the shock talking. "It will be okay. I'll stay with you every minute. I'll get Mom to stay with your sister."

She tugged at his shirt, bringing his face next to hers, pulling his head down to her mouth. "Reed will hurt her if I go to the cops," she breathed in his ear.

He clasped her to him. "They can protect you. I will protect you."

The new phone she'd gotten after her release from jail buzzed and she pulled it out of her pocket. Her hands shook so badly she almost dropped it, but the message on the screen drew a gasp from her.

Turning the screen to Owen, she showed him. "He must have gotten my cell phone number from Candy."

It was a photo of Betsy. She looked perplexed, confused. The text that accompanied it was only two words: so easy.

"Don't let him intimidate you," Owen said. "The cops can trace this phone number, find his DNA here." But even as he said it, Owen knew the flimsy promise his words carried. Reed could be sending the photo from a disposable phone. He'd likely been smart enough not to leave prints anywhere.

The house phone rang and both women jumped. "I'll get it," Owen said.

He snatched it up, half hoping it was Reed.

"What are you doing in my sister's house at this hour?"

Owen huffed out a breath. "Hey, Ray."

"Don't 'hey, Ray,' me, Marine. What are you doing there?"

Though the tone was jovial, the question underneath was not. Ray didn't want a former marine, especially a former marine fighting a painkiller addiction, having a relationship with his sister.

While he was contemplating how to explain what had just occurred, Ella reached past him and took the phone.

"Ray," she said. "He was helping me get the front door open, that's all."

In actuality, he'd been unable to sleep and he figured a drive by Ella's place might help him visualize how Reed had managed to pull off killing Baker and planting the body in Ella's van. Owen cocked his head at her. "Tell him," he mouthed. He knew why she didn't. Ray was half a world away and his work required his full and complete concentration. Worrying about Ella might compromise his own safety. Still, he thought. Ray had a right to know.

She held the phone between them so Owen could hear Ray's next question.

"Are you sick? Got a sore throat or something?"

"Yes," she said. "My throat does hurt at the moment."

"So the legal thing is okay, then? You're out of jail and Owen's taking care of getting your case overturned, right?"

"I'm doing my best," Owen said.

"I'm trying to arrange some leave, but it's taking a while."

"Betsy and I are okay," Ella said, blinking back tears. "Thanks to Owen."

"Yeah, well, don't get too cozy with that jarhead," Ray said.

"Nice, coming from a fellow jarhead."

Ray dropped the teasing tone. "We make bad partner material. You know that and so do I."

Owen felt a stab of pain. Ella's kiss resurfaced in his mind.

I'm built for war.

You're made for more than that.

Ella was talking, trying to pry info from her brother who was giving her everything but the serious details that no deployed marine would think of burdening their loved ones with. She kept one hand pressed to her throat, as if to ease the pain.

"I gotta go now, Ells," Ray said. "Take care of yourself and Betsy and I'll get back as soon as I can. Give the phone to Owen, would you?"

She did.

Owen pressed it to his ear.

"I'm trusting you, man," Ray said. "Get her out of the mess and keep them safe until I get home."

"I will," Owen said.

"That's what I needed to hear."

"Keep your head down, Ray."

"You too, brother."

The call ended and he hung up the phone.

Ella was chewing her lip, pacing the floor. Every few laps she would stop at Betsy's wheelchair to smooth her sister's hair or straighten the blanket over her knees.

Ray had reminded him of the crux of the mission.

Keep them safe. Period.

He would not be distracted by ricocheting emotions.

End of story.

NINE

It took all Ella's remaining strength to convince Owen that she would not involve the police.

"He will kill her," Ella said. "I saw the truth in his eyes." Her own eyes burned with tears that she held in check through force of will. The marks on her throat would not prove anything to Larraby who had already decided she was guilty. The only option, her only choice, was to somehow save herself, and if she could not do that, at least she would go to prison knowing that Reed had no reason to harm Betsy.

Frustrated, Owen had finally stalked outside to make some phone calls after she made him promise he would not involve Larraby against her wishes. She tried sipping some ice water to ease the ache in her throat. Betsy had gone to bed for the night after Ella had promised to lie down with her as soon as Owen left.

"The bad man isn't going to come back," she assured her sister, praying that it was true. Her skin crawled at the memory of his touch, his delight at her powerlessness, the crush of his fingers squeezing the air out of her.

Owen came back inside.

"You're coming to stay at the ranch. Barrett and Shelby are away so you and Betsy can stay in Grandad's cabin."

She goggled at him. "Owen Thorn…"

He stared at her. "Don't even bother to argue, Ella. You're not staying here with a busted door and no help for miles."

"But…"

He folded his arms across his broad chest. "But what?"

"You're treating me like a child."

"I'm pulling rank."

"You're not on active duty. You don't have a rank."

He lifted a shoulder. "Once a marine…"

"Always a marine, I know," she groaned.

"Let your pride take a back seat to common sense for a minute. You know I'm right."

Hands on hips, she glared at him. "Well, aren't you supposed to ask a woman what she wants rather than tell her how it's going to be?"

"If I'd asked, would you have agreed?"

She sighed. "No." It irritated her to no end that he was right. "I can't impose."

"You're not. We've got sixty horses that need

your help, remember? You're still on the books as our farrier, last I looked."

It made her feel somewhat better to know that she would be contributing at the Gold Bar in some small way. "I can't yank Betsy out of bed. She's finally gone to sleep."

"We'll leave in the morning, then. I'll stay and take the night watch."

"That's not…"

He ignored her, sitting on the couch and putting his feet up on the fruit crate that served as a coffee table, the rifle across his lap. "Don't mind me. I'm just going to relax and watch The Weather Channel. Won't even know I'm here."

And how was it possible she could forget that there was a gorgeous, stubborn cowboy with a loaded rifle doing MP duty in her living room? Though she would never admit it to him, she was secretly relieved. "Who watches The Weather Channel for relaxation?"

"Me. Grandad used to say the weather always gets its way. Did you know that the fastest a raindrop can fall is eighteen miles per hour?"

She sighed.

"I've got more weather trivia. Want to hear it?"

"No."

"The low is expected to be in the twenty-degree range tonight."

"I am not going to change your mind, am I?"

"That's an affirmative." He grinned and then

he sobered, blue eyes earnest, compelling. "Ella, we are going to prove Bruce Reed guilty."

She started to protest, but he held up a palm.

"If you don't want to go through the police, I will respect that. We can make this a covert mission if you want, but we're going to win. He's going down and you and Betsy will be safe."

He sounded so rock-solid certain that a tiny corner of the fear lifted.

She grabbed a blanket from a basket and handed it to him.

He laughed at the raggedy patchwork squares. "I remember when you made this your freshman year in high school. For a home economics class project, right?"

She smiled. "Yeah. I didn't get a very good grade because the seams are crooked."

He chuckled, draping it across his shoulders. "I like crooked. Straight seams are overrated."

She sighed. "That's exactly what you said to me the day I was crying over that grade."

"I know," he said softly, "I remember." In the dim light the blue of his eyes turned to liquid silver and she felt lost in their luminosity.

And suddenly the sweetness of their shared childhood past seemed to wash into the present, the same, but different. Owen Thorn, her companion, was now a grown man ready to put his own safety and future on the line for hers. Did he feel the same quickening of the pulse? The odd sensation that their relationship was both old and brand new?

No. He'd always been the protective, loyal best friend of her brother.

Semper fidelis. Always faithful.

That was all and that was enough, she told herself.

"Good night, Owen," she said.

The next morning, Owen drove Betsy and Ella to the ranch, stopping in front of Grandad's cabin. Knowing his mother, she'd probably checked to be sure the place was in the same pristine condition it had been in when Grandad was alive. There was already a ramp in place, so moving Betsy in her wheelchair was no problem. He made sure she had everything she needed.

"Meeting at twelve hundred hours in the kitchen," he told her.

"What meeting?"

He gave her a wink. "Battle plans."

She sighed. "Why do I feel like I've just enlisted?"

He handed over the box of tools.

"What's this?"

"Ran into Zeke in town yesterday. He meant to give you this when he loaned you the truck. Said you can return them when you get yours back. There's an apron and an anvil in the barn too."

She accepted the farrier's box tenderly, as if she

was taking the hand of a small child. He could tell she was fighting tears that she did not want him to see. "You don't... I mean, your family doesn't have to let me work. I don't want to be a charity case."

He stopped her then, tipping her chin up with his finger until he looked into those anguished eyes, sparkling with tears. "Hey," he said quietly. "You are the best farrier we've ever had on the Gold Bar. Do you think we'd let just anyone work on our horses?"

She did not smile. He allowed his fingers to graze the silk of her cheek, to skim tenderly over her bruised throat. "I heard from Zeke that you were recruited to work for the farrier team for the Olympics a while back. You never told me that."

She shrugged. "I declined the offer. That's all there is to say."

"Why? It's been your dream to work with champion horses like that."

"God's plan was better for me than my own."

He cocked his head, puzzled.

"It's not important right now," she said. "I'd be happy just tending to the horses in this town, if anyone still wanted me."

"We want you, same as we always have." *I want you*, his heart unexpectedly supplied. Startled, he took his hand away.

"Rocky's thrown a shoe and we've got three that

need hoof trimming," he said breezily. "Whenever you can get to it."

She lifted her chin. "Betsy's inside helping your mother. I'll start right now."

He grinned. "I figured you would. See you at lunch."

He watched her walk to the barn, lugging the heavy box, though he did not dare offer to help. Ella Cahill was holding onto her life with both fists, clutching as hard as she could to keep it all from slipping away. It made him burn with pride and determination.

"We'll beat this, Ella," he said. "You have my word."

Ella held Rocky's hoof between her thighs, the split legs of the leather apron allowing the perfect grip for her to pry off the old shoe and begin trimming the frog and cleaning the sole. Then came the nippers to cut away the excess hoof wall. When the horseshoe was properly adjusted to her satisfaction, she nailed on the new shoe.

She gave Rocky a rub on his spotted sides. He nickered softly and she imagined he was saying, "Thanks, kid." Three more to go, she told herself, relaxing for the first time since her ordeal had begun. There was no other place in the world where she knew she belonged, knew that she was doing what God intended for her, than when she was tending to horses.

And no one's going to take that away from me, she said to herself as she finished up with Rocky.

Though she wanted to finish her trimming duties, Owen summoned her for lunch. They gathered in the Thorns' kitchen, Betsy proud of having set the table and Mrs. Thorn handing around sandwiches and bowls of savory vegetable soup.

"Where's Keegan?" Owen said.

"Here." Keegan sported the ever-present grin, black hair falling across his forehead. "Sorry, took me a while to get Barrett's chores done along with mine."

"Wash up and sit down, honey," Mrs. Thorn directed. "We're about to say grace."

"Yes, ma'am."

Owen's father led them in a simple prayer of thanks, which echoed in Ella's heart. She was profoundly grateful that she was sitting in the crowded kitchen with her sister, about to enjoy a meal with people who were not tainted by suspicion of her. The gratitude lasted until fear took its place. What if she never saw any of the Thorns again except for prison visitation? What if she could never prove her innocence? Suddenly her appetite was gone.

"Eat, Ella," Mrs. Thorn said, grasping her forearm. "Stay strong to face these troubles."

Mrs. Thorn knew a thing or two about troubles, having lost her first daughter-in-law to a drunk driver. She'd always managed to encourage Ella to attend their family gatherings when her own father was on his cross-country trucking jobs and she was left alone with Betsy. Somehow it had never seemed like charity, or pity. Mrs. Thorn had a way of making people feel loved, not just taken care of, and that was a gift from God—she was sure of it.

Keegan wolfed down a couple of bites of his sandwich. "So what's the game plan? I haven't been able to find that thermos, even with the metal detector."

Ella sat up straighter. "Wait a minute. I just thought of something. It's Tuesday, right? It's my day to work at the Gregory's ranch." She blushed. "Macy Gregory hasn't canceled me yet, anyway, unless it slipped her mind. I'm working on Trailblazer today."

"That's her new jumper?" Owen asked.

Ella nodded. "Macy lives and breathes to jump horses."

"While her husband, Drake, tends to the real stuff, like keeping a working cattle ranch afloat," Keegan put in, ignoring a pointed look from his mother. "Heard he didn't want her to buy Trailblazer in the first place since she bought and sold another jumper just last year that never even ribboned in a competition. They had to sell off some stock to bring in some cash."

"That's their business," Tom Thorn said.

Ella grew thoughtful. "Macy hasn't been satisfied with Trailblazer's performance and I've seen Bruce Reed there a few times looking him over with Macy. It seemed like they knew each other well," Ella mused. "I'm going to go over and see if she still wants my farrier services. Maybe she'll talk to me about Reed."

Owen put down his napkin. "I'm coming too."

"Keegan and I will keep looking for the thermos," Jack said.

"Good plan," Keegan said. "Mrs. Gregory is not my biggest fan. She won't forget about me flying my drone helicopter too near her property."

"That was nosy and as I recall, we grounded you for three months," Mrs. Thorn said.

Keegan grimaced. "Longest summer of my life. I missed the rodeo and everything, but that was years ago, anyway, and I apologized."

"Best for you to keep clear. And Betsy and I," Mrs. Thorn announced, "will do some cyber-sleuthing."

Everyone stared at her.

"What?" she said, taking in their surprise. "You don't think I have it in me to be a detective?"

Keegan laughed. "The way you used to ferret out when I'd cut school or gotten into a fight? You're a regular Mrs. Perry Mason."

"No," Tom said. "She's a Mrs. Tom Thorn. Let's keep that straight."

The laughter echoed through the kitchen, mingling with the warmth from their shared meal. Though she did not dare put much stock in it, Ella could not help but feel the tiniest flicker of hope.

TEN

Owen idled the truck a minute along the approach to the Gregorys' Three Stone Ranch. In the distance, Drake Gregory sat astride a quarter horse amid a sea of cattle. He sighed. There was nothing so beautiful as watching a good cow horse at work, the instinctive way they could anticipate the movement of the herd, their fluid grace in singling out an animal from the rest. It was truly a partnership between cowboy and horse. It took Owen's breath away every time.

Drake was in the saddle, focused on his task, oblivious to Owen's truck. Owen admired his ease, knowing his own leg would be screaming at him. He'd never admit it to any living person, but his riding stamina was still not what it had been, even after a long year of rehab. He suspected his brothers knew, as they always seemed to turn up with a job for him when he was pushing himself too hard. Their pity left a bitter taste in his mouth.

Gonna get it all back, he told himself again. *Almost there.*

Ella put a hand on his arm. "Okay?"

"Yeah, sure," he said. "Admiring the horse. I'm almost done working with Glory, for Drake. Hoping she'll be just as good as his others."

"She will be, if you're training her."

She said it so matter-of-factly, but pride flushed his cheeks. How did she do that? Make him feel like a whole man again with just a couple of words. He wanted to thank her, to hold her hand and let the feelings spill out, that fragment of fear that would not dissipate no matter how hard he worked, how much he prayed. Instead he drove the truck to the stables and parked.

Jaw set, Ella got out with her tools.

Macy Gregory was on the phone, forehead creased, shoulders tensed. After a moment, she must have heard some good news because she relaxed, huffing out a breath that ruffled her short, gray-streaked hair.

When she saw them, she clicked off the phone.

"I didn't expect to see you here," she said to Ella.

"It's Tuesday." Ella flashed her a smile. "I'm here to take care of Trailblazer."

"No need for that," Macy said.

"Please, Mrs. Gregory. I didn't have anything to do with Luke's murder. You've got to believe me."

She took off her glasses and polished them with the bottom of her T-shirt. "It's not that easy."

"Yes, it is," Owen said. "Bruce Reed is trying to frame Ella for murder."

Macy stared at him. "Got proof?"

Ella cocked her head. "No," she admitted. "Can you tell us how you met him?"

Macy looked in the distance toward the field where her husband was working the cattle. "I met Bruce a few years back in San Diego when Drake and I were…on a break. It wasn't…you know, a good time in my life."

"Did Reed try to get money out of you?" Owen said.

She winced. "I never let it go that far. Drake's a good man, even though he's hard to live with. He can't stop thinking about ranch business for one single moment." Her mouth crimped. "But he's always been like that, so why would I expect any different?" Her gaze went hard. "Sometimes I think he loves those horses more than he could ever love me."

Owen shifted, uncomfortable to have this glance into the Gregorys' marriage. He cleared his throat, not sure he wanted to hear the rest. "So you met Reed?"

"Yes. I was at a horse auction, looking at some animals that my husband complained we couldn't afford, and we bumped into each other."

Right, Owen thought. More likely, *Reed tar-*

geted you for a lonely, vulnerable woman. Macy must have picked up on his thoughts.

"Believe it or not," she said, "my head was working fine, just not my heart. He wined and dined me. It was fun, flattering and he shares my passion for jumping, unlike Drake." Her mouth clamped in an unforgiving line. "Anyway, Reed knows his horses."

"Did he advise you to buy Trailblazer?" Ella asked.

Her eyes narrowed. "Yes. I got Trailblazer through a connection of his. Not unusual. Linda Ferron over in Rock Ridge did too. Reed knows how to connect people with the horses they want."

"For a nice cut of the action, I assume." Owen said.

Macy frowned. "Your mother taught you to be polite, Owen. What happened?"

Owen did not break eye contact. "I don't want to cause you embarrassment, Mrs. Gregory, but Ella's life and future is on the line. Reed is targeting her, framing her for Luke's murder, and that's got to stop."

"I'm sure Reed didn't have anything to do with that. He's after Luke's aunt, after all." Her eyes flashed. "Or her millions, anyway, so why would he kill her nephew?"

"That's what we're going to find out." Owen settled his cowboy hat against the breeze. "He advised you to buy Trailblazer. Are you happy with the horse?"

She looked away. "Ella knows, she's been around enough. Trailblazer was inconsistent. One minute he was nailing the jumps and the next he'd refuse. It drove me crazy."

Ella nodded. "You were hoping to work through it."

"Well, I didn't. Not champion jumper material, but that happens sometimes. That's the horse business. It was a mistake, an expensive one."

Owen pressed. "You didn't get the horse you paid good money for. That must be frustrating, since you bought and sold a jumper just a year ago."

"Thanks for reminding me." She shrugged. "You have to put out in order to find that one-in-a-million champion. I wish my husband understood that."

Drake was no doubt more concerned with keeping the Three Stone solvent than indulging his wife's expensive hobbies. *Their business,* he reminded himself.

"I have things to attend to," she said, still not looking at them.

An alarm sounded somewhere in Owen's gut. *She's lying about something, and she's not going to tell us any more.*

"I'm happy to see to Trailblazer while I'm here, Mrs. Gregory."

"No, Ella."

"Please. You don't have to pay me and I understand you want to find another farrier, but it will take time and he needs his hooves trimmed. At least let me do that one last time."

Macy turned impassive eyes on Ella. "I meant that you can't take care of Trailblazer because he's dead."

The words fell like stones.

"He died a few hours ago."

Ella's mouth dropped open as she tried to process Macy's bombshell. "What?"

"You heard me," she said.

A strong, healthy horse? Dead? As Ella was struggling to process, Zeke Potter came out of the barn, brow furrowed. He nodded to Ella and Owen.

"Can't explain it," he said. "One of those things. Colic. He didn't have a chance."

Ella had seen horses suffer with severe colic and it was a horrific thing to watch. Horses had such delicate digestive systems that a simple gastrointestinal upset could progress to full-blown intestinal strangulation or impaction, which could lead to an excruciating death. It happened, so why was she having such a hard time believing it had happened to Trailblazer? Her heart ached for the passing of that playful, beautiful creature.

Macy continued. "He was distracted when I

took him out this morning but not pawing or rolling. Heart rate and rectal temp were good and I listened to his gut. Everything sounded normal. I stabled him to keep an eye on him, withheld food, water and all that, but I had to tend to some things in the house. When I came back, he was dead. I called Zeke, even though there was nothing he could do."

Drake walked over to them, face sweaty and grimed. "Doc?"

Zeke blinked hard. "I'm sorry, Drake, but Trailblazer's dead. Colic."

Drake didn't react outwardly, but Ella saw the sheen of regret in his eyes. The man loved horses, all of them, even Trailblazer, though she suspected Drake had probably been against the purchase of another expensive horse that wasn't of the working variety.

He took off his hat and scrubbed a hand over his beard. "Macy..."

"Don't start," she snapped. "You'll be happy to know that Trailblazer was heavily insured. I just put in the claim. I have to arrange to have his body disposed of, so you can rant at me about my bad investment later."

He shook his head. "Was gonna say I'm sorry about your horse."

She looked at the ground, mouth pinched.

Drake muttered something, crammed his hat back on his head and said a curt goodbye.

A truck pulled to a stop and Bruce Reed got out. Fear flashed through Ella's senses and she might even have run if Owen hadn't wrapped an arm around her shoulders.

"Steady," he breathed in her ear. "He's not going to touch you."

Her lungs were not up to the job of breathing, only Owen's rock solid presence held her together.

Reed did not seem surprised to see them there. "Ella," he said, taking a step forward.

Owen pulled her behind him. "Not one foot closer."

Reed sighed. "You've got too much of the alpha male thing going on, Mr. Thorn."

"You touch her again and you'll find out exactly how much alpha I've got going on."

Macy watched them, eyes narrowed. Tension roiled off Owen in hot waves that Ella could feel through her jacket.

Reed held up his palms. "I don't know what she's told you all, but I'm no threat to Ella."

His audacious lies set her nerves on fire. The bruises throbbed where he'd almost squeezed the life out of her. She wanted to tell Macy and Zeke exactly what Reed had done, but his threat to Betsy was an ice pick in her gut. *So easy. I can make anything look like an accident.*

"Of course," Macy said. Ella did not miss Macy's sarcastic tone.

Ella tried to pull Owen away. "Let's go. Macy

doesn't want my farrier services anymore. No reason to stay."

Reed's expression turned saccharine sweet. "Lost another job? I'm sorry, Ella. That must make it real tough for you, what with a cripple for a sister."

"She's not a cripple, she's a woman with a disability," Ella hissed. It made her furious when people identified Betsy by her physical condition, especially this lying, scamming monster. "And her mind is better than yours."

He laughed. "No offense intended." He focused on Zeke and Macy. "I heard the horse is dead."

"How'd you hear that?" Owen asked.

Reed shrugged. "News travels fast in a podunk town."

Zeke sighed. "You heard right. Shame."

Reed lifted a shoulder. "Fortunately, you had it insured, Macy. Plenty of funds to get another now."

"Funds? Is that how you look at a horse?" Ella could not hold back.

"That's exactly how he sees them," Owen snapped. "Just like he looks at people. A means to an end."

"Careful, you two," Reed said, eyes sparking. "That almost sounds like defamation of character." There was a silver of malice in his tone and she read it loud and clear. *Continue and you risk your sister's life and your own...*

"All right," Macy said. "I don't have time to listen to any more of this. I've got to make arrangements for Trailblazer."

Ella had no desire to spend a moment longer in Reed's presence so she picked up her farrier box and marched toward the truck, hoping that Owen would follow. He did, but before they reached it, his phone rang. He yanked it to his ear while she struggled to get her emotions under control.

Reed lounged against the corral fence, talking to Zeke, but she had a feeling he was tracking her every move. Determined not to be cowed, she deposited her borrowed gear into the back of Owen's truck.

"Yeah?" Owen's cheeks were flushed and his body still telegraphed that he was amped from their encounter with Reed, but whatever was said over the phone stopped him. "We're on our way." He drew her close and spoke low in her ear.

"Jack found it."

Blood pounded in her throat. "My thermos?"

"Yes," he said. Grabbing her close, he swept her into a hug that lifted her off the ground. "This is the break we've been waiting for. Now the battle's going in our direction."

A swirl of hope kindled in her belly as his arms tightened around her waist. Could it be so easy? "Where? Who?"

He lowered her to the ground, moving to the

passenger side and opening the door for her. "I'll explain on the way."

Ella shot a quick look at Reed as they left. His stare penetrated to her core as he watched them drive off the Gregory's ranch, like a wolf tracking a rabbit.

ELEVEN

Owen recapped his phone conversation as the truck rattled back to the main road. "Jack's got a buddy, Pete, who is a crazy fisherman. He's always got his hook in the creek whether there's anything to be caught or not. Jack put the word out he was looking for your thermos."

"And this Pete actually found it?"

"Yep. He's tent camping about six miles from here."

"Six miles? How could it have made it there?"

"The place where you were…um, the spot where I found you was near the creek, remember? It rolled down to the water. Creek's full to bursting right now so it got carried along."

She shook her head. "Impossible."

"Nah," he said, eyes sparkling blue as a robin's egg. "Things are breaking our way for a change."

"I'm afraid to believe it."

"Believe it," he said, taking her fingers and squeezing her hand. It was such a tender gesture, so full of kindness and something else. Balm to her soul, ease to her tortured spirit, until she remembered she was supposed to be keeping Owen and his family out of harm's way, not bringing them into the line of Reed's fire. Running into Reed had probably worsened the situation for both of them. Still she could not bring herself to withdraw from his touch.

"Jack's already on his way. He'll meet us there."

"I'm almost too excited to breathe."

He laughed. "Keep breathing high on the priority list, okay?"

"Do you think... I mean, is it safe to leave Betsy and your family for so long without you and Jack, and Barrett out of town?"

He nodded. "Trust me. Keegan's the most dangerous of us all, and my dad was an MP in the army. He knows how to handle himself." Owen smiled. "Come to think of it, my mom is a force to be reckoned with if she feels her family is being threatened. When I was a kid she faced down a mountain lion with a shovel when my dad was away."

She laughed. "I remember Jack telling Shannon and me that story once..." She stopped abruptly.

Owen shot her a look. "It's okay. I know Shannon was your best friend, in spite of the fact that she crushed my brother's heart."

"She still is my best friend, even though she's in Los Angeles. At least, I think so. We used to talk every week but lately she hasn't returned my calls." She didn't mention that Shannon's last phone call had been hurried, tense, with the clamor of the emergency room where she worked filling the background.

"Yeah, Oscar told me when I dropped a pie off at the inn that he missed seeing his niece at Christmas."

"I'm sure she's just busy. Her emergency room internship and all. I know she helps at a battered women's shelter too."

He nodded. "Yeah. That must be what it is, just busy."

"Has Jack… I mean, has he finally accepted their breakup?" Jack Thorn had been a different person when he was dating Shannon Livingston seven years before. She'd never seen him smile so much, socialize as much as he had when they were together. How had things fractured between them? Shannon had not been able to disclose much without breaking down in sobs that had wrenched Ella's heart. Only recently could they talk without her asking about Jack. Did he seem happy?

Owen considered. "I don't know how Jack's handled it all. He's gone from quiet to nearly silent. He doesn't say much, but he's the best listener in the country, I'm pretty sure." A shadow flickered over his face. "Listens to all my whining."

Ella stroked his fingers. "Betsy's heard plenty of my complaints too."

He shifted. "I've been thinking. I didn't realize how much… I mean, how difficult things must have been after both Ray and I left."

"Never looked back, did you?"

He sighed. "No, I guess we didn't."

"Now that you know what a struggle it's been for me and Betsy, would you have made the decision not to enlist?"

He hesitated, mouth working, and then he spoke. "I would have gone anyway. I'm sorry."

She surprised herself by laughing, reaching over and kissing him on the cheek. "There now. That was an honest answer. You haven't ever lied to me since I was a freckle-faced kid and that's worth something in this world."

"Well, that doesn't quite make up for Ray and I leaving you here alone, does it? It wasn't fair."

"My father used to say that we don't get fair on earth, only in Heaven. I could have handled things better." Her face burned. "I acted out. Humiliated myself and endangered Betsy. I'm sure you've heard."

He kept his gaze trained straight out the front windshield but his fingers tightened around hers. "I heard after I got back. Not gonna get condemnation from this guy, believe me."

She blinked hard. "Thank you, but I've come to peace with it, mostly. God forgave me so it's okay for me to forgive myself."

He swallowed.

"He forgives you too."

"I've got a few more sins on my plate than you, Ella."

"Not more, just different."

"I know He forgives, but sometimes I still feel like I'm being punished. I can't…" He blew out a breath. "I can't do what I want to do. Not yet anyway. This leg."

"Someone told me taking up your cross and following Jesus means you sometimes say no to what your heart wants."

"That's painful."

"Excruciating, like experiencing a death."

He looked closer at her. "Is that how you felt when you gave up the chance to work with the Olympic Team?"

"I gave up that dream because He wanted me to be here with Betsy. And yes, it hurt like crazy, but you know what? It's been better than I could have ever imagined."

"I don't know if I'm that brave."

"Not sure it's bravery," she said. "But I know it's the life God meant for me to have."

He breathed out, shaking his head. "But giving up your heart's desire. I mean, when I picture myself hobbled forever, not being able to go back…" He stopped abruptly.

She fought down a stab of shock as she realized what was deep in his heart. "Owen, are you hoping to return to the marines?"

He stayed quiet, confirming the truth. Her stomach felt like the bottom had just fallen out of it. It shouldn't surprise her. Being a marine gave him purpose and passion, just like her brother. He would leave again as soon as he could. And why not? What would keep him here anyway?

An unexpected pain cut through her heart, but she didn't let go of his hand. Instead she exhaled slowly and caressed his fingers. "It's okay."

Owen's expression was troubled.

I'm made for war.

And he would leave to go chase after it. Leave her. Before it would have made her angry. Now, she felt only sadness.

Owen was relieved when they crossed the old wooden bridge and pulled off the main road, following his brother's directions. His own behavior startled him. He'd never actually uttered aloud the craving of his heart, to return to the marines. He was not sure why he had told Ella, and why exactly she hadn't informed him he was crazy, selfish, unrealistic or anything in between. He probably was all of those things.

They got out into the chilly afternoon and took the winding path down to the creek. The first couple of feet were difficult until his leg finally unlocked a bit. Ella was walking so fast he could hardly keep up with her. Shadows bathed the woods and the sound of the swollen creek was deafening the closer they got. They met Jack and a portly middle-aged man with a full shaggy beard covering his face.

"I'm Pete," the man said, shaking their hands. "I knew I was gonna make a great catch today."

"You always think that," Jack said, "even when you snag nothing but branches."

"Yeah, well, I caught me something today, didn't I? Good thing you told me to keep a look-out." He held up the plastic bag with the thermos inside. "Better than trout, huh?"

Owen held his breath while Ella looked at it. How cruel would it be if it was not her thermos Pete had found. "Yours?"

She nodded, face alight with a smile that made his senses swim. "Yes. See? You can still see some of the sharpie on the bottom where I wrote my name."

She flung her arms around a startled Pete. Owen was surprised at his pang of jealousy. *Get it together, Owen, you dolt.*

"Thank you," Ella said. "You might have just saved my life."

Pete grinned as she let him go. "Well, then, I guess it don't matter if I catch any fish today."

"I'll buy you a fish dinner," Owen said. "All the trout you can eat."

Pete laughed. "I'll take you up on that sometime."

Ella took the bag. "Do you think there will be traces of the drug inside or any fingerprints left?"

"We'll take it to the cops right now," Owen took a picture of the thermos for good measure. "It's four o'clock, so we'd better hustle."

"Keegan's gotta go pick up a horse," Jack said. "I'll go back to the ranch to cover."

Jack often sensed Owen's unspoken moods, and right now Owen was concerned that Bruce Reed might try something while he was not at the ranch to prevent it. He'd seen eyes like Reed's before, flat, not revealing any emotion, not even hatred, eyes that promised death to whomever got in the way. He'd rather deal with an enemy's out-and-out hatred than a sociopath who had no feelings at all.

"Yeah. Good," Owen said. "Be there as soon as I can."

Without another word, Jack turned to walk back along the trail. Ella caught his arm and took his hand in hers.

"Thank you, Jack."

Owen saw him look at her small white hand against his sleeve and for a moment Jack's face was so wounded, so agonized, he knew his brother must be thinking about Shannon, remembering a time when they'd walked hand in hand.

"Sure," he said, striding off toward his vehicle, shoulders bent against the cold.

Sometimes you say no to what your heart

wants...and it feels like a death. Jack had done exactly that.

He allowed himself to think for a moment about giving up his beloved marine corps. *It sure does.* But Owen was not ready to give up anything just yet, especially not the corps.

They loaded up in the truck. He noticed that Ella was shivering so he set the heater to full blast and waited a few minutes for the vehicle to warm. The temperatures had dipped into the forties as the sun set and there was a promise of frost.

He pressed the gas a little harder, considering the extra time he'd need to prep the horses for such a cold night. The current batch they cared for was hearty and hale, most with sufficient winter coats to weather the chill just fine, but there were two older horses with more delicate health that were used to being turned out at night, and he decided it would be best to blanket them. The other one, Linus, had not been eating well, and Owen determined he would do best with an extra dose of TLC. He was lost in the details as he drove up the steep road that would take them away from the creek.

Behind him, an old SUV pulled out from the sharp turn.

His muscles fired to life and he stomped the accelerator.

"What?" Ella gasped. She turned to look behind them. "Oh no. How did he find us?"

Tony, Candy Silverton's stable guy, gunned the engine and began to close the distance between them.

TWELVE

How? her brain screamed, but it was not so hard to figure out, really. Reed had seen Owen take the call, must have realized something was afoot by their hug and sent his lackey to follow them. Reed was desperate to stop them, which meant the thermos was a threat. Small comfort if they were both killed by Reed's crazy henchman.

She clung to the door as the truck careened along, the SUV closing the gap with every passing second. Each foot of rough road jostled her so badly she bit her lip and tasted blood. The seat belt jerked hard against her ribs, anchoring her in place.

"Gonna try to make the bridge," Owen said, fighting the wheel. "He won't make a move after we get back to the main highway."

She screamed as the SUV slammed into their back bumper, sending the truck skidding. It crashed against the boulders that lined the road with a hair-raising groan of metal on rock. Ella thought for sure they would be crushed, but Owen managed to wrench the wheel and get the truck back under control.

"Take my phone," he shouted to her. "Call Jack."

She attempted to dial but Tony slammed into them again from behind and the phone flew from her hand. She dared not try and retrieve it, instead scrambling for something to hold onto.

Owen floored the gas pedal and the truck flew like a rocket toward the two-lane bridge. She agreed with Owen's plan. Once they were through, the road would empty out onto the highway where there would be other cars, witnesses, help. No one, not even a crazy man like Tony, would attempt to waylay them there. They were almost to the entrance, but Tony was so close she could see him in the side mirror, mouth set into a grim line that matched Owen's. His knuckles shone white on the steering wheel.

Owen's truck surged ahead onto the bridge and her spirit soared. "We're gonna make it," she wanted to holler, but at the last second Tony made one final desperate bid. The fender of the SUV loomed in the mirror and he rammed the truck again with such force that Owen's front end was driven into the wooden rail of the bridge.

The old bridge beams moaned in protest against the impact. In slow motion horror, she saw them splinter and buckle. One jagged beam punched through the windshield as Owen's truck tore into them. Flinging herself to one side, she barely avoided being impaled as the wood pole bisected the space between her and Owen. There was no way to stop their momentum. Her stomach flipped as the truck skidded through the ruptured structure. In a dizzying spiral, it careened over the side of the bridge, plummeting downward toward the swollen river.

There wasn't time to scream, to cry out.

Owen raised his arm towards her as if he could somehow keep her from falling along with him into the icy water.

Two seconds ticked by.

The truck struck the water with a hammer blow that rammed the air from her lungs, driving her back against the seat back so hard she thought her neck would snap. Her arms and legs flopped uselessly as if they were made of rubber.

For a moment it seemed they were going straight to the bottom until the pickup popped back up to the surface so fast her senses were dizzied. They were floating. She could hardly believe it. Owen's hand still gripped the wheel, the other clutching the beam that had nearly killed them both.

Another two seconds, three. Her mind started to piece together what had happened, but her body refused to do anything but suck air in and out in frantic rhythm. The truck lurched forward and the fractured front window ushered in frigid water that began to fill the cab as the vehicle spun in slow circles.

Owen grunted, turning toward her. Her throat caught at the sight of the blood flowing from his hairline down the side of his face.

"Get out. Now," he said. He undid his own seat belt and fumbled for hers, but she was already free of it. She struggled to push the door open but it would not budge. He tried his side, straining with the effort.

"Too much water inside," he called over the roar. "Gonna have to wait until it rises and the pressure equalizes."

Panic filled every pore. There was no way she was going to sit quietly and wait until the rising water covered her head. It was already lapping at her waist and moving up. She kicked at the door, shoving her shoulder against it as hard as she could, but Owen was right—it did not budge.

Water swirled in now nearly to her collarbones, robbing her of warmth, freezing her senses until her arms and legs grew numb to the point of uselessness. The only thing she could feel was naked fear. What if the door didn't open? The thought of watching the water creep up to snuff out her life nearly made her scream. To compound her terror, it was getting dark. Trapped in the gloom, she was waiting for the water to rise up to fill her mouth, nose, lungs. She thought of Betsy. Who would explain it all to her?

He grabbed her hand. "Another minute."

She squeezed his fingers as they both endured the longest sixty seconds of their lives. The icy touch of the water seemed to press out every sensation but her mounting panic. When she thought she could not hold back the scream, Owen tested his own door and found that it slowly gave. She let out a squeak of relief. The level was now up to her chin and she fought to breathe in the small pocket of air between the water and the roof.

He crammed himself into the space above the dashboard so she would be able to climb over the beam and squeeze past him. Grabbing the thermos from her, he shoved it in his waistband. "Water's moving fast. You're going to need both arms free. Take a breath and swim for shore. I'll hold the door open until you're clear."

"I'm not leaving you."

"I'll be right behind you. Remember when we were kids? Last one to shore is a rotten egg." His grin was forced. The blood from the gash in his forehead was still flowing. Death hovered moments away, or maybe it waited for them somewhere out in the freezing dark water. They were not kids and this was not a game.

She reached for him. "We're going together."

He grabbed her wrist. "No. I'll follow. On three, you're gonna swim out. There's a green light on the dock across the river. Head for that and don't stop. One…"

"Wait," she said.

"Two." He was pulling her toward the door.

Owen, no, she wanted to say. *We do it together or not at all.*

He suddenly took her face in his palms and kissed her, mouth cold on hers, but somehow warming her anyway. When he pulled away, his eyes were intense, wide with emotion as he brushed a thumb over her trembling lips. "Make it to shore, you hear me?" His voice was tight.

"Owen…"

"Make it to shore," he repeated.

"Not…"

"Three," he said, yanking on her wrist.

She found herself shoved out into the swirling water. The pounding grip of the current caught her up immediately. She tried to anchor herself in place, to fight against the pull until she saw for herself that Owen had made it out of the submerged truck. She did not have the strength to beat the current. The tumult smothered her cry as she was sucked farther and farther away from Owen.

Owen lost sight of her as soon as she cleared the vehicle. Breathing prayer after prayer that she would make it to shore, he kicked off his boots and pushed out after her. The grip of the water nearly turned him over, but he broke the surface, sucking in a lungful of air. The setting sun sent shadows across the rushing waves, and he thought he saw a glimpse of her head several yards ahead. He struck out.

Owen had been an excellent swimmer in his day, but now his body was cold, blood blinding him and his weak leg working against him. The energy seemed to leach out from his muscles but he kicked on. Pausing to rest was not feasible as he could not hold himself still in the torrent.

Had she made it? He didn't dare look again, just kept kicking and drawing on every ounce of marine training to keep moving toward that tiny green light. His leg and hip were a fiery torment that sapped his remaining energy with each awkward kick. When he thought he was done for, that he could battle the sucking water no longer, the river began to shallow out under his feet.

Inch after excruciating inch, he half swam, half crawled to the gravelly shore, clawing at fistfuls of the riverbed to move himself along. Flopping onto the ground he lay there, exhausted, coughing up water, trying to rally himself enough to sit up.

Ella…

The thought forced him upright, head spinning. He was relieved to feel the bulk of the thermos in its ziplock bag still stuck in his waistband. Ella's hope for a future was still secure. He pulled it out, scanning for her.

"Ella?" he yelled. He heard nothing, but the

roaring current might have drowned out any reply. He hollered again several times before he stopped.

The green light shone a couple of meters to his left. She must be there, waiting for him. Other scenarios jostled in his mind but he pushed them aside. She was ashore, cold but unharmed. She had to be.

He forced his cramping muscles into action and began the trek to the green light. Trees on the bank crowded down almost to the water, and he stumbled over exposed roots as he made his way along. Shadows danced along the ground and he felt exposed, vulnerable, as if he was clearing houses in the Helmand Province without his rifle or body armor. Tony might have made it across the bridge and be biding his time.

Skin prickled along the back of his neck and he whirled around.

Nothing there. No Tony. He shook his head to try and clear his hearing, but his ears still rang from the sound of the impact, the roar of the river. He pressed on, his foot catching on yet another protruding root.

Muttering, he straightened in time to see the iron hook arcing toward his neck.

THIRTEEN

Ella's eyes burned from searching the darkness for Owen. Had he drifted farther downstream? Her darkest fear reared like a troubled horse. Had he not been able to escape the water at all?

"I never should have left him." Her throat was tight, but she forced her shivering limbs into motion. She would keep looking for another few minutes before she risked running to the highway to flag down help. It was fully dark now, and only the moonlight aided her in her search.

A shout ripped through the night. To her left? She started running, heedless of the uneven ground that made her stumble. There on a patch of moonlit ground were two figures locked in a violent hold. Owen? Even as she tried to take it in, he went down on his back, Tony standing over him, hand raised.

Her heart thunked to a stop as she saw the gleam of the metal hay hook raised to pierce Owen's chest.

"No," she screamed, just as Owen's foot shot out to sweep Tony's legs from underneath him.

"Cops are on their way, Tony," she screamed, running to Owen. "Get away from him."

Tony grabbed at something near Owen's legs and Owen did not move to stop him. Then Tony sprinted away into the trees. Ella ran to Owen and sank to her knees.

"Owen," she breathed. "Thank goodness. I thought you'd drowned." When he did not answer, her relief turned to fear. She peered closer. His eyes were open, one arm flung wide and the other tucked against his body. "Where are you hurt?"

He did not respond.

"Owen, where are you hurt?" she breathed.

He still did not reply, but his lips moved.

She put her face to his. "Tell me."

"I'm sorry," Owen whispered. "He got it."

"What? What do you mean?" Owen winced as if seized by a sudden pain. She understood. The thermos. Tony had gotten the thermos, her only proof, her only chance.

Fighting down a wave of despair, she pressed her palms to his cheek. "Never mind that now." Her fingers brushed his neck and he groaned. Squinting in the poor light, she saw the bloody gash where the hook had found his shoulder. She took off her jacket and pressed it to the wound. "We'll get you to the hospital," she said, voice quavering.

How exactly? His phone was gone but hers was

still in the pocket of her jeans. Eagerly she yanked it free. Maybe, just maybe, it would still function.

One look told her it was beyond salvaging—not even the flashlight would function. She put his hand to the jacket. "Can you press here?"

He attempted to do what she asked and she grabbed him under the arms and tried to drag him. He cried out in pain before he clamped his lips together. Owen was a big man, much bigger than her one hundred ten pounds, and although she was strong from years of arduous farrier work, she had not been able to move him more than a few inches. Panting, she realized the only way to save him was to make it to the road for help.

She knelt next to him. "I have to go get help," she said, stroking his cold cheek. "I'll be back in a few minutes."

"Don't come back," he whispered. "Tony might return. Go to the ranch. Stay safe. My brothers will come for me."

She pressed her forehead to his. "No man left behind," she said, tears coursing down her cheeks. "I'm just as tough as any marine. Don't you know that by now?"

The corner of his mouth quirked in a flicker of a smile. "I'll be right back and you will wait patiently until I get here, understand?"

"Affirmative," he said.

She didn't allow herself to think anymore. She ran, scrambling up the rocky bank, pulling herself along until she made it to the green light that marked the end of the dock. Clambering up, she saw the headlights coming straight at her.

Tony? Or help? Her nerves screamed at her to take cover but Owen was bleeding down on the shore and she did not know how long he could last.

She waved her arms. "Help me."

The driver door opened. Pete got out. "What happened? Heard a crash and saw the truck go into the river. Jack's gone downstream to search. Where's Owen?"

She almost cried in relief. "Can you call an ambulance? He's hurt. Down there." She pointed. Pete frantically dialed his cell phone, grabbed a blanket from his truck and they scrambled back to Owen.

His eyes were closed, but he stirred when Ella stroked his face. "Help's here, Owen," she said. "Hang on, okay?"

He didn't answer this time.

She stayed with him, holding his hand, trying to chafe some warmth into his body. It seemed to her that the bleeding had slowed, but she could not be sure. Jack and the ambulance arrived almost simultaneously, Larraby only minutes behind.

She filled them in while Owen was loaded into the ambulance.

"I'll put out an APB on Tony," Larraby said.

Anger overrode her self-control. "Now do you believe me that Bruce Reed is a criminal?"

Larraby was impassive. "Right now we have to find Tony if we're going to tie anything to Reed. Can you walk me through what happened one more time?"

"No," she snapped, "I can't. I'm going to the hospital to be with Owen."

Without another word, she turned her back on Larraby and got in the truck with Pete. Jack had already gone ahead. As much as she hoped Tony would be arrested before dawn, she could not turn her thoughts away from Owen. He'd been her friend, her ally since she was seven years old. He could not die.

He could not die.

Owen swam to consciousness to find himself in a hospital, strapped to a table. A doctor stood above him with a hypodermic needle.

"No," he barked, struggling to sit up.

The doctor jerked and the nurses pushed him back onto the table. "It's okay, Mr. Thorn," the doctor said. "You got on the wrong end of a hay hook. We've given you blood, and I'm going to stitch you up."

"No narcotics."

The doctor stared. "Just enough to get you through this, son. Hook went in pretty deep."

He swallowed hard. "I can't."

A long moment passed. The doctor's gaze

drifted to the blankets where he must have examined Owen's mangled leg and guessed the rest.

He lowered the needle. "Okay. Some topical pain relief only. We can give you prescription strength ibuprofen for after. It's going to hurt, I'm afraid."

Couldn't hurt worse than a painkiller addiction, he thought. He wanted to ask about Ella. Fuzzy memories of her kneeling over him on the riverbank floated through his mind along with a fact that was too upsetting to be imaginary. He'd lost the thermos—her only chance. He'd been too slow, too weak, and that punk Tony had taken it from him as easily as stripping away a kid's lunch money on the playground.

He closed his eyes as the doctor washed something over his wound and he willed himself to sleep through the pain that was coming.

It didn't work. He endured the procedure as best he could, refusing to cry out. They installed him in a bed in a cramped room. His mother and brothers came in. He searched behind them but Ella was not there.

"Family only, they told us," his mother said. "Your dad is tending to Betsy."

His mother stroked his hair and checked the bandages to be sure they passed her strict quality control. She did not cry. She'd seen her boys through every kind of injury from broken wrists to him getting shot in the line of duty, to Keegan's litany of wounds, to the death of Barrett's wife, and in every case, she'd closed her eyes, thanked God that her boys were still alive, and tended to the practical matters at hand. Women were strong, he marveled, and his mother was the strongest of them all. She displayed her quiet calm now, ticking off a list. "We'll bring you some clothes from home. When you're better, you can use Barrett's truck since he's still gone."

"And we're going to find Tony." Keegan's eyes glittered dangerously.

"Leave it to the police," he said, but he knew Keegan would let his anger lead the way. He was not sure he wouldn't act the same if one of his brothers had been attacked, but Keegan had a wild spirit and scars from his childhood that had yet to heal. He shot a silent look at Jack. *Keep him out of trouble.*

Jack acknowledged with the barest lift of his chin and Owen felt a surge of gratefulness. Jack was shouldering the load for everyone at the moment. It galled Owen that he had not been able to deal with Tony himself. He resolved then and there to see his physical therapist again, to demand to know the truth. Could he get healed and go back to the marines? Could he be enough again?

But what of Ella? And why did that thought cause him pain when he'd deployed so many times before without a backward glance?

His family pulled him from his uncomfortable

musings until he could not hide the pain, which he desperately did not want them to see.

Jack noticed. "He needs to rest. We should go."

His mother kissed him and prayed over him. Keegan gave him a curt nod. "We've got this, Owen. Rest up."

Jack waited until the others had left and slid a new cell phone onto the tray table next to him. "Our numbers already programmed in. We got Ella one too, same cell number as before."

"I won't be here long," he called to his brother as he left.

Jack quirked a smile. "I know. Nurses will be begging us to get you out of their hair within the hour."

He sighed. "Ella?"

"She's okay. Refused the doctor's exam. Stubborn. Go figure. Mom brought her some dry clothes and Dad put her on the phone with Betsy."

"Thanks, Jack."

He didn't answer as he left Owen to his pain.

FOURTEEN

Ella tiptoed to Owen's bed and the sight of him lying there scalded her heart.

Because of you... He's here because of you. What if the hook had caught him an inch to the left, landing deep in his artery? Trembling started up in her muscles. She'd never thought of it before, never allowed herself to consider the dangerous work he'd done, the very real possibility that he might never come home again. And now her situation had almost cost him his life here in the States. How would it feel to lose Owen forever? Her throat went dry until she comforted herself with the steady rise and fall of his wide chest.

He was alive, and she thanked God for it. She could not resist grazing his stubbled chin with her fingers, stroking the old scar that just showed along his cheekbone. She startled when his eyes opened, blue as a summertime sky.

"I'm sorry. I didn't mean to wake you."

He blinked. "What time is it?"

"Five fifteen or so."

"A.M.?"

"Uh-huh."

"Tell me you haven't been here all night, Ella Cahill."

She shrugged. "Okay. I won't tell you."

He groaned. "Go home to Betsy. Get some rest."

"Stop bossing. I had to wait until the coast was clear to sneak in and see you. They've got some family-only rule except during certain hours. I tried to explain we've known each other since grade school, but they don't give credit for that."

He smiled and took her hand. "I do." Then the smile faded. "I'm sorry I lost the thermos."

"You didn't lose it. Tony took it, at Reed's request, I'm sure." She forced a brave tone. "I'll find another way."

"We...we'll find another way."

She shook her head. "No, Owen. I'll deal with it. I don't want you getting hurt for me again."

His hand tightened over hers. "Don't do that."

"Don't what?"

His eyes flashed blue heat. "Don't treat me like I'm some wounded child. I'm a man. I make my choices and I'm choosing to be your second on this thing."

"Are those cowboy rules or marine rules?'

He pulled her closer until she could feel his

warmth, the intensity that shook her. "They're my rules," he growled.

His body was battered and bruised, but the pride still shone bright and clear. The enemy bullets that carved up his leg also struck a near-lethal blow to his self-image. But he'd powered his way past a painkiller addiction with God's help, and she could not allow him to think her concern was out of pity or that he was anything but the strong man she'd always known him to be. She stayed silent. He caressed her hand.

"Sure you're okay?"

She nodded. "Yes."

"I never want to have to explain to Ray that I let you get hurt."

The words doused any warmth she'd been feeling. Of course. He was Ray's best friend, beholden to his marine brother to protect her. The kiss they'd shared in the truck, was just an aberration, born from a moment of crisis.

She was his duty, nothing more.

Don't you forget it, Ella.

Shoving back the hair from her face, she got up and looked out the window, fighting back a sudden urge to cry.

He wriggled higher on the pillow. "Doc says I can go home Thursday, but I'm aiming for today, soon as my mom brings me some clothes."

"I won't even try to argue. It's like trying to

stop a tank with a squirt gun." She was relieved he'd unwittingly returned her to solid ground. *Why did you let your heart wander anyway?*

He laughed. "Smart."

Yeah, smart, and that's what she had to be to help herself, her sister. Time was ticking away until she would lose Betsy, her freedom—everything. The door opened and Ella sucked in a breath. Candy Silverton stood there looking as shocked as Ella felt.

"What are you doing here?" Candy hissed, her white-blond hair impeccable. The heavy makeup accentuated the lines around her mouth and eyes and did not quite conceal the shadows of fatigue.

"Visiting Owen," Ella managed.

"It's family only," Candy said.

"Then why are you here?" Ella shot back.

Candy raised a penciled eyebrow. "I get what I want. When you donate a million dollars to the hospital, you're everybody's family. Get out before I call security. I want to talk to Owen."

"She stays," Owen said. "Due respect, Miss Silverton, you're wrong about Bruce Reed. He's trying to destroy Ella and I know that guy was involved in your nephew's death. Truth is, I think he murdered Luke himself."

She sucked in a breath. "I won't listen to that. It makes no sense anyway. Bruce loves me and Luke was my only family."

"And your sole heir?" Owen's voice was low but the insinuation sounded loud and clear in the small room.

"Until I…" She flushed. "If I marry, of course I will amend that so my future husband will be taken care of, but there is no way Bruce would do anything to hurt me. Since I met him last year he's done nothing but shower me with affection, help me purchase horses…"

"Did you have them appraised?" he asked.

"Of course. Someone from the insurance company came out and Zeke Potter is going to examine them too. If you don't believe me, ask him."

"But that's been delayed, hasn't it? And you haven't gotten a thorough look at them either yet, have you?"

She looked away.

"It's Reed's pattern, Miss Silverton," Ella ventured. "Luke told me he was doing some digging and he found that Reed had many relationships with vulnerable women, getting them to buy horses worth less than the paying price while he lined his own pockets with the profits."

"What other women?" Her lips trembled. "Tell me names. I know he helped Macy Gregory, but that was purely out of friendship." She folded her arms. "Go ahead. What names, Ella?"

The flush crept up her neck. "He didn't get a chance to tell me."

"Before you killed him, you mean."

"I did not kill him," she said through gritted teeth.

Candy glared at Ella. "You have nothing to back up your claims, but it is an indisputable fact that you borrowed money from my nephew and didn't pay it back, correct?"

"I was almost ready to repay that loan." She recognized the inadequacy of the words that sounded lame in her own ears. It shamed her again to admit her precarious financial condition in front of Owen.

Candy sniffed and turned her eyes to Owen. "Listen, I just came to apologize for my stablehand. I heard that Tony went crazy and attacked you and I feel terrible about that. He wasn't that great a worker, but I had no idea he'd go this far. I should have fired him weeks ago."

"He attacked me to steal evidence that would incriminate Bruce Reed," Owen said.

She gaped, hand fluttering to the scarf at her throat. "I can't believe that."

"You've got to, Miss Silverton," Owen said. "Bruce Reed is…"

"A wolf in sheep's clothing," Ella finished softly. "Those were your nephew's exact words."

She looked from Owen to Ella. "I'm leaving."

"Wait…" Owen called, but she had already

stridden out the door. He sighed. "She can't stomach the truth."

Ella swallowed a stab of pity. She understood how Candy felt. Hoping for that sweet, unconditional love that forgave all things, endured all things? How tantalizing it was to imagine, and Candy thought she'd found that in Reed. Reality was a bitter pill to swallow.

Finally she realized Owen was staring at her. "You sure you're okay, Ella?"

"Yes." She took a breath. "I have an idea about who I need to talk to next."

"We. Who we need to talk to," he said, mouth hard. "Who?"

"Linda Ferron." She saw his wheels turning as he tried to recall the name.

"The woman Macy Gregory mentioned."

"Yes. She said Reed had some connection with her too. She's local, in Rock Ridge somewhere. If I dig a little, I can track her down." She held up a hand when he protested. "I mean, *we* can track her down. She might not have anything to tell us, but then again…"

"She might. Okay," he said, as if to get out of bed. "I'm coming with you."

"You're not getting out of here until a doctor says so anyway."

His eyes narrowed. "And you think you're gonna stop me?"

She poked a finger into his chest. "Just try me, marine."

His mouth twisted in a look caught between annoyance and amusement as he eased back on the bed. The white of the pillow set off the brilliant sapphire flash of his eyes.

Hospitals were not the right place for Owen Thorn.

Smothering a heavy dose of guilt, she left.

Beside himself with aggravation, it was nearly dinnertime when Owen finally made his escape from the hospital. Though his mother had delayed bringing him clean clothes, he suspected as a means to keep him in the hospital, he found a way.

"Thanks, man," he said to Leonard, the hospital orderly and former marine who'd loaned him coveralls, retrieved his boots for him and given him a ride back to the Gold Bar.

Leonard saluted. "Semper fi, Captain."

Owen saluted back, though it set off a circuit of pain in his shoulder. "Maybe it will take your mind off your leg," he muttered to himself with some acid as he let himself in the house.

Keegan looked up from the paper he was reading and checked his watch. "Twelve hours and sixteen minutes. You stayed in longer than I thought. You're slipping, bro."

"Where's…?"

"Right here," Ella called from the family room. She was sitting with Betsy, helping her hold a thick pencil. "B-e-t-s-y," she spelled out as she helped her sister trace the letters onto white paper. "That's really good. You can practically do it all by yourself."

Betsy nodded, bending to write the letters again without her sister's help. He sank into a chair, biting back a groan and watched them, wondering why Ella made a point of teaching her sister the laborious lessons, until a long forgotten memory resurfaced. As a seventeen-year-old, he'd driven his mother to visit an elderly lady who had become too bedridden to go to church. She'd tended to the woman's basic physical needs and then to his great surprise, his mom asked him to help position her in front of the piano. She settled the gnarled fingers on the keyboard and sailed on with a piano lesson as if it was the most natural thing in the world. He'd asked her afterward.

"Mama, isn't it kind of pointless to give her piano lessons now?"

"She wants to learn."

"But…"

"We don't get to decide what people's limits are, Owen. I'd much rather be a bridge than a door."

A bridge rather than a door. As Ella encouraged her sister, her long red hair glinted in the firelight. She'd turned away from some of her dreams for her own life to be that bridge for Betsy.

The unselfishness of it made his mind boggle. He thought again of their shared kiss in the truck. Why could he still feel it long after the moment was over and gone? But clearly it had not affected her in the same way. He realized she'd drawn near, waiting for him to answer.

"I'm sorry. What did you say?"

Ella smiled. "Just the usual 'how are you feeling' questions which you're going to avoid anyway."

Now it was his turn to smile. "I was going to say I'm…"

"Happy, pleased and proud," she cut in. "You and my brother both said that for every occasion, whether things were falling down around your ears or not."

"Doesn't pay to complain."

"No, I guess it doesn't." She patted his forearm and her soft touch drove away the pain for a split second. Ella's attention was drawn at a grimace from her sister. She hastened to adjust the cushion, her lip between her teeth.

"I'll get you a new one as soon as I can," she whispered low, but Owen caught the words anyway.

His heart cracked a little. She didn't have the money. She had no more steady income from her job and he doubted the meager insurance she had covered extras like the wheelchair cushion.

You'll have a new one, he silently promised Betsy. *And your sister won't have to beg for help as soon as we get her name cleared.*

His mother came in with a basket of laundry and sighed. "Owen Matthew Thorn, you are the worst patient that hospital has ever seen."

"Yes, ma'am."

She placed the laundry basket on the coffee table and bent to give him a kiss on the forehead, her quickened breath negating the sternness of her tone. "I thought it would get easier when you were back in the States. Wrong again."

"I'm sorry," he said. *Sorry I worried everyone, sorry I was slower than Tony. Beyond sorry I lost the thermos.*

"Never mind, honey." She bustled to the kitchen and returned with a bowl of potato soup. "Eat something. You look pale."

He spooned some up with his left hand to avoid straining his wounded shoulder, hoping he would not spill. It gave him a new appreciation for Betsy's efforts to subdue her uncooperative muscles. Tough, those Cahill women. Ella brushed the hair from her face, revealing the soft curve of her cheek.

And lovely too.

Jack joined them, handing his mother her laptop. He nodded at Owen, showing not the least surprise that his brother had discharged himself.

"Now," his mother said, powering up the laptop, "shall I tell you what Betsy and I have discovered?"

FIFTEEN

Ella was tickled at the look of pride that shone on both Evie and Betsy's faces. Betsy might not fully understand what was going on, but she knew she had helped and that was enough.

"We've been doing some digging on Bruce Reed," Evie said as Tom came in to listen, holding a cup of steaming coffee and settling next to Owen.

"Good to have you home, son," he said.

Owen closed his eyes and exhaled. "Good to be here, sir."

Pain grooved lines into Owen's forehead and she wished again she had not drawn him into this dangerous cat-and-mouse game with Bruce Reed. If Reed had sent Tony to retrieve the thermos at all costs, she felt certain there was nothing he would not stoop to. There had been no word from Larraby. Tony had not been apprehended. Tony and Reed were two dangerous threats, in addition to the trial, which loomed ever closer. The sound of the jail cell door clanging shut echoed in her mind. Fear clogged her throat.

Evie continued. "I'm not the greatest investigator, of course."

"You always managed to sniff out the trouble I got into no matter how much I covered my tracks," Keegan said.

Owen raised an eyebrow. "She just followed the smoldering trail of destruction."

When the chuckles subsided, Evie continued. "There wasn't much finesse involved in our cyber sleuthing, I'm afraid. We just searched Bruce Reed's name and read every tidbit we could get our hands on about the man. It is positively scary how much information is out there, cluttering up the internet."

Ella's stomach went tight, desperate to know what Evie had discovered.

"We stumbled across a few facts. First off, his real name is Dale Reed—Bruce is his middle name. He was raised on a farm in Ohio, which apparently he detested according to a biography I'll get to in a minute. There's a reference here and there, he left Ohio and eventually worked as a bus driver and he was involved in an altercation with a passenger over which he lost his job. Apparently, the passenger made some crack about him being short and Bruce threw him down the steps and onto the sidewalk."

Keegan snorted. "Definite anger management issues."

Evie nodded. "But here's the juiciest bit."

Ella found her hands were clasped tight together. She forced herself to relax.

"I read this part aloud a couple of times to Betsy and showed her the picture. She indicated it was the same man who entered your house."

The feeling of his cold fingers pressing on her throat made Ella swallow hard. *So easy.*

"It's a biography included in a newsletter. It indicated that Reed started working at a stable in Colorado, first as a groomsman and then teaching riding lessons. There's a little paragraph bio about all the instructors and the pictures too. Here's what it says. 'Bruce Reed was one of eight children raised on a goat farm in Ohio, but tending to livestock left him wanting more. He moved to Boulder, Colorado, where he met and married Violet Wilder, a fellow horse lover. He has assisted at the prestigious American Gold Cup and the Saratoga Classic Horse Show competitions.'" She looked up from the screen. "But here's the interesting thing. This was an old archived copy of a spring newsletter, but when I looked at the summer issue, his biography had been deleted and replaced with someone else, so I surmise he didn't work there long."

Tom drummed fingers on his coffee cup. "Those are esteemed horse shows mentioned in there. The grand prize for the Gold Cup is $250,000. Think he really assisted with those?"

"Not in an official way, but maybe attended to get close to women with money," Jack said, startling Ella. "I think he drops names, implies connections that he doesn't have to work out his scams."

"Like he's doing with Candy Silverton? Talking her into buying the six broodmares?" Keegan said.

"Maybe Candy's the top prize," Jack said. "If he can actually get her to marry him and gain access to her millions." He frowned. "That is, if he's really no longer married to Violet."

Ella stood and began pacing. "I'll talk to Zeke. He was supposed to arrange to see Candy's new mares. He'll be able to tell us if she was duped."

"And we've got the name Linda Ferron," Owen put in. "We know she's local and Reed had dealings with her. Maybe she can help us with some intel."

"I found a reference to her sister who runs a trailer park in Rock Ridge. I figured she might be able to tell us how to find her."

"Tomorrow…" He squirmed in the chair.

"Maybe," Ella put in. "Let's see how you feel in the morning."

"You already know how I'll feel." His eyes danced with a mischievousness that warmed her inside. "Happy, pleased and proud."

Keegan yawned. "And sore, let's not forget that

one. I can go with Ella and talk to Linda if you need some downtime."

"No way," Owen said. "You have the tact of a charging bull."

His eyes opened wide in mock irritation. "I am offended."

"And there's another trail to follow now." Tom nodded to his wife. "Right, Detective Evie?"

She giggled. "Yes, now that you mention it. We need to find Reed's wife, Violet. I'm hoping they're divorced since he's galloping after Candy Silverton." She frowned. "In any case, she has to know enough about his character to give us something to take to the police."

He nodded. "You've got the place they were married. Going to do some records searching?"

"Yes, I am." She looked at Betsy. "Will you keep me company tomorrow while I search?"

"Yes," Betsy said, and although it was garbled, the one small syllable brought tears to Ella's eyes. Every word was precious, every small indication that Betsy was all right made all of Ella's struggles worthwhile. *It's going to be okay,* she wanted to tell her sister. But they were still a long way from proving Ella's innocence.

And if Bruce Reed had his way, they never would. The thought hitched her breath. But the warm glow from the fireplace illuminated the faces of Tom, Jack, Keegan, Evie and Owen who would all stand up to Bruce Reed to keep Ella and her sister safe.

Thank you, God, she thought, blinking back tears, *for this family.* She noticed Owen was looking at her, his face bruised, obviously his body ached, but there was something infinitely gentle in his expression as he gazed at her.

Cheeks warming, she reminded herself that Owen was helping her because of Ray and a nostalgia about their shared childhood. What's more, he would be right back to his marine corps family the moment he could spare her from prison and get his body to cooperate. Duty done, mission accomplished.

She flashed on an image of her father returning home from his long-haul trucking assignments, eating eggs and toast, listening sober faced as she reported on her school progress, on Betsy's health status, on their church attendance, their lives communicated in neat information briefs. He wanted the facts ticked off like the items on a duty roster. She'd wanted assurance, approval, encouragement, all the myriad emotional desires not delineated on his checklist. He loved her, she did not doubt it, but since he could not be what their mother had been, nor even the type of father she craved, he settled them each into categories, with jobs to be done, reports to be given. It was the only way he knew. She'd bottled up the words that threatened to bubble out.

Why can't I just be a regular teen like my friends?
Why can't I have fun and enjoy life like they do?
Why can't you ever say, 'I love you'?

Sometimes she still wondered, but God had given her a choice. *Follow me and give up the life you think you should have because what I offer is so much richer.*

And it was. Ella knew that truth in every one of Betsy's smiles, in the satisfaction she felt at caring for her sister, the joy of living in Gold Bar, tending to her horses, being a part of a community.

Was that sweetness gone now? Would her reputation always be tainted by the shadow of what had happened?

Owen quirked a reassuring smile at her, as if he knew what thoughts were churning inside her. She sent a smile back, brighter than she felt.

We'll get this mission done, Owen, and you'll be free to go. No guilt, duty done. With only a small tug in her heart, she wheeled her sister back to tuck her in for the night.

Owen fought his way out of bed the next morning, grateful that he'd slept better than he'd expected. Maybe that was the benefit to enduring chronic pain—a person learned how to appreciate the small respites whenever they came along.

A hot shower loosened up his muscles and he was inspired to phone his physical therapist to schedule an appointment for the following week. The secretary seemed surprised to hear from him.

"Have you suffered another injury, Mr. Thorn?"

How much time have you got? "Not to my leg. I want to talk to Dr. Von about reenlisting." There. Second time he'd said it aloud. His new resolve filled him with hope.

"I will relay the message." She scheduled him for an appointment. Energized, he strode cautiously out to the kitchen ready to tackle their mission.

Find Linda Ferron and get the dirt on Bruce Reed, enough to bury the slimeball for good.

Ella was already in the kitchen, eating some toast alongside her sister. The paper covered with scrawls indicated they'd already had their morning writing lesson.

He tapped the paper. "Good job, Betsy. Your handwriting is better than mine."

Betsy smiled and he was gratified to see it. Ella's hair was pulled into a twist, her jacket and a small pack in her lap.

Evie came in and shook her head at Ella. "Toast? Not even an egg or a slice of bacon? That's not going to keep body and soul together."

"I don't want to cause you any trouble, Mrs. Thorn."

"Scrambling an egg is not trouble. Look, see?" She held up a basket. "Trixie and LouLou are still laying even in the thick of winter. I've got eggs and you two need a real breakfast, so sit."

Owen did as he was told. "A cowboy takes orders from his mama," he said with a smile. "If he knows what's good for him."

In a few minutes the four of them were sitting down to scrambled eggs, fluffy and golden, and strips of crisp bacon.

The kitchen phone rang. Owen waved his mother back into her seat. "I'll get it."

The voice on the other end was muffled. "Keep out of my business or you will all regret it."

Owen's chest tightened. "Is that you, Bruce? Why don't you be a man and admit it."

The color drained from Ella's face. She stood, staring, hands to her mouth. His mother got up and looped an arm around her shoulders. Keegan and Jack came in, stopping in the doorway to listen.

"You heard me," Reed snarled. "No more chances."

"So you're resorting to the stalker-on-the-phone thing?" Owen snorted. "Coward. If you want to hold someone responsible, blame me because I'm gonna dig up every bad thing you ever did and wave it like a flag for all the world to see, including Candy Silverton. This whole town will know you're a liar and a con man and someday we'll prove you guilty of Luke's murder too."

"You can't touch me."

"Oh, I'm going to do more than touch you. You're going down. Ella Cahill and her sister are family and you crossed the wrong people."

The line went dead and he replaced the phone in the cradle.

"What should we do?" Ella breathed.

"Find Linda Ferron, just as we planned. We'll start in Rock Ridge like you suggested."

"But…" she said, shooting a worried glance at her sister.

Jack pushed off from his spot on the wall. "We're here, and we're going nowhere today."

Keegan nodded, eyes glittering dangerously. "Personally, I'd love to see Bruce Reed show up here. It would just make my whole day."

Evie gave Ella's shoulder a final squeeze. "We will not ask for trouble," she said, eyeing her youngest son, "but if he shows up here we will protect ourselves and Betsy."

Ella gulped in breath. "I guess… I mean, unless I decide to give up…"

"Which you won't," Owen said.

"Then the only way to get out of this mess is…"

"To push through the threats and bring Bruce Reed to his knees." Owen went to the closet and retrieved his rifle. His brothers would have theirs primed and ready also, he knew. As cowboys on a ranch with a thousand acres to protect, they were ready to handle anything from coyotes to bears to intruders and anything in between, and they'd do it in a heartbeat to protect the family.

Semper fidelis, always faithful. It applied just as much to the Thorn family as to his marine brothers. He clapped on his cowboy hat and led the way out the door.

SIXTEEN

Before they left town, Ella called Zeke and turned on the speakerphone. He answered on the first ring.

"It's Owen and me, Zeke. I wanted to ask if you got a look at Candy Silverton's horses."

"Her new broodmares? Oh, sure."

"I'm surprised because Tony was moving them away from the ranch Monday morning."

"Yeah. Reed said something about the paperwork hadn't cleared and Candy couldn't take possession right away. I met them at a ranch over in Littleton and looked 'em over. Nice bit of horseflesh there. She should get her money out of the young'uns."

Ella's heart sank. "So Reed didn't cheat her into buying worthless horses?"

"Not with these six," he said.

She blew out a breath. "Okay, well, maybe this deal was legit, but be careful, Zeke. Reed is a wolf. The less you have to do with him and Tony, the better."

"I know a thing or two about wolves, Ella. Corner them and they'll sink their teeth into you. Maybe the best way is to make him understand you're not a threat. He's a businessman, first off."

Anger boiled inside her. "He's a con man and he murdered Luke and he's threatened me and my sister."

Zeke was silent a moment. "Then you need to be careful, do what you have to do to keep Betsy safe. Back away from him, Ella. I don't want to see you get hurt."

Zeke Potter was the dearest man she knew, but he was hopelessly naive. "I can't back away. If I do, I'll go to prison for murder."

"It won't come to that," he said.

She sighed. "Zeke, I know you never want to see the bad side of people. Just promise me you'll be careful."

"You should be the one doing the promising, young lady. Remember what I said about wolves."

Corner them and they'll sink their teeth into you. She clicked off the phone.

Owen took her hand. "A minor setback."

"But I was so sure he was inflating the mares' value and skimming money off the top for himself."

"We'll find out more from Linda Ferron." He pulled her fingers into his and squeezed.

Butterflies danced in her stomach. "How can you be so sure this bunny trail will lead us to the truth?"

"If it doesn't, we'll find a new lead to follow, but Reed's phone call this morning is a show of desperation, which means we're getting close."

"I thought we were close with the thermos." His grip tightened.

"I've been thinking about that. If Reed has the thermos, why would he bother calling the Gold Bar and spouting off threats? I wonder if it's got him rattled that the cops are on the lookout for Tony. Maybe he fears that Tony will spill his guts if he's caught."

"Or Tony might be hiding out somewhere with the thermos, intending to blackmail Reed with it."

Owen grinned. "Couldn't happen to a nicer guy. Kinda awesome imagining Reed experiencing some stress, isn't it?"

She laughed. "I suppose you're right, but why don't you let me drive?"

"'Cuz you're a lead foot."

"I am not and your shoulder's hurt."

"It's okay and I'm driving. Anyone who keeps a row of horse bobbleheads on the dashboard of their van is not to be trusted with transportation needs."

Owen did not have so much as a paper clip cluttering the pristine interior of the truck he'd borrowed from Jack. "By the way, I'll have you know, Owen Thorn, that you gave me two of those horse bobbleheads."

"I did?"

"For my fifteenth birthday."

"Oh, that's right. I'm surprised you kept them."

"They're my two favorite ones."

"That right? I…uh… I mean, I thought maybe you might have thrown them away after Ray and I left."

"I would never throw away something you gave me." Warmth crept up her neck and she knew she must be blushing. Silly of her to hang onto toys from her childhood.

He wriggled the wallet out of his back pocket. "Now that you mention it…take a look under the license."

She peeked under the worn leather flap and fished out a half-inch purple wooden heart. Stunned, she remembered inking the piece with Magic Marker. "I gave you a Purple Heart before you left for boot camp."

"Because you said if I already had one, then I wouldn't go and do something foolish and get myself hurt and earn a real one."

She sighed. "It made sense at the time. I didn't know you kept it."

"Went with me on every single mission." His voice went hoarse. "Even the one when I went ahead and earned myself a real Purple Heart."

Her pulse kept time to the beats of silence that passed. "I wish you had never earned that one."

"Me too, but I did and I lived to tell about it, and I'm gonna recover fully, which is more than I can say for some of my guys." He gripped the steering wheel, lost in the horror and grief.

She touched the little wooden piece, a tangible reminder of her childhood innocence, her affection for Owen that was now fledging into feelings which she could not box in, no matter how hard she tried.

"Besides, if I hadn't gotten myself shot, I wouldn't be here with you now."

Her pulse pounded until he finished the thought.

"Helping you out of this mess."

She looked out the side window to give herself some time for composure. "I would have figured it out myself."

"Yeah, but I guess God wanted us to do this together."

"I guess He did." In spite of everything—her wounded pride, the lick of resentment, her strange desire to have more with Owen than he was willing to give—she was grateful that he was there beside her.

Gently, she slipped the wooden heart back into his wallet and he returned it to his pocket.

They arrived at the River Gorge Trailer Park just before lunchtime. Owen held his breath and kept quiet as Ella inquired in the trailer park office. He figured the gray-haired woman behind the counter would be more likely to answer the questions of a sweet, freckle-faced redhead than those posed by a banged-up gorilla like himself. The place was sour with the smell of cigarette smoke.

The lady took a sip from her bottle of bubbly water. "I'm Linda's sister, Dory. What do you want to see her for?"

Ella's posture straightened a notch and he knew she was as excited as he was at having found a possible lead. "I need to know about Bruce Reed and I believe Linda knows things about him."

"Things?" Her grizzled eyebrows narrowed into an angry line. "She learned about him the hard way, in spite of anything I had to say, but then, she's always been like that—thinking she knows better than anyone else. She'd been smarter, more successful than me until she met Bruce Reed. Then she got her comeuppance."

"Can you tell me what happened?"

"Why are you interested again?"

Ella took a deep breath and let it out. "To be perfectly honest, Dory, Reed is targeting me and he's threatening me and my sister. I need to find some evidence to bring him down before he destroys us both."

The words died away into ten seconds of perfect silence before Ella added, "Please, can you help me?"

A quick struggle flared across Dory's eyes until she shook her head. "No, I don't want to have anything to do with Bruce Reed. I don't need trouble."

Ella's shoulders fell and Owen limped forward to put a strengthening hand to her back, his leg having tightened up during their ride. "We really need your help, ma'am," he said quietly. He pointed to a picture on the wall in a marine uniform. "That your boy?"

"Yes. He's deployed to Camp Dwyer and I count the days until he comes home." She cocked her head at him. "You in?"

"Yes, ma'am. Returned home last year."

"That where you got the limp?"

"Yes, ma'am," he said, keeping his eyes on hers. "A souvenir from my deployment."

She took another sip of the bubbly water, thoughtful. "I'm not going to tell you anything about Bruce Reed because I'm not sure what's fact or fiction, but you can ask my sister yourself. She lives in the last trailer, nearest the creek."

Score one for the team, Owen thought. "Thank you, ma'am."

"Don't thank me." Dory hesitated. "I've never had much fond feeling for my sister, but she didn't deserve what happened to her so you're gonna be nice, aren't you?" It sounded more like a threat than a question.

"Yes, ma'am," he answered, and Ella nodded. "We will not upset your sister unnecessarily."

They left the office and walked down the paved road, bordered on each side by trailers with well-kept pots of flowers. A few curious residents offered friendly waves, which they returned.

"They probably think we're a couple looking to buy here," Owen said.

Ella blushed.

For a second, he wondered what it would be like if it was actually true, if he and Ella were a couple, starting their lives together. That would mean he had given up the dream that sustained him.

But if taking up your cross meant giving up your own dream to take the better life that God offered...

The thought both scared and confused him so he put it aside as they found the last trailer. It was set apart from the nearest one, concealed by a cluster of dense shrubbery that cried out for a good pruning. The sound of a burbling creek met their ears and the scent of moist ground hung heavy in the air. Striped curtains covered the windows and he could not stop the urge. He drew Ella behind him.

She gave him a puzzled look, but did not question. He might not have been able to explain anyway. They were here in the good old US of A, but the sense of being watched, targeted, would not be ignored.

He stood to the side of the door, Ella behind him, and knocked.

SEVENTEEN

Ella felt the tension radiating off of Owen as he rapped on the door for the second time.

"Ms. Ferron? Your sister told us you might be able to chat for a minute," he called.

The trailer remained dark and quiet until a slow shuffling sounded from the other side of the door. It opened a few inches and a woman with thinning, straggly hair peeked out. Her thick glasses were askew on her nose and her breath smelled of alcohol.

"What do you want?" It was hard to guess her age, probably somewhere in her midfifties, but she might have been much younger. The lines on her face told the story of her difficult life.

Ella stepped around Owen. "I'm Ella Cahill. I'm a farrier, and this is Owen Thorn. He works a ranch in Gold Bar." She handed over one of her business cards to add some credibility.

Linda peered at the card. "Don't need a farrier at the moment."

"We need to talk to you about Bruce Reed," Ella said.

"Bruce Reed." She twirled the name around in her mouth as if she was tasting it. "Bruce Reed."

"Yes," Ella repeated. "Do you know him?"

"Oh, yes," she said, eyes shifting. "I know him. Come on in." She turned away and disappeared into the house, leaving the door ajar for them to follow. Something deep inside Ella did not want to enter that dark space, but her feet took her in anyway, following just behind Owen.

The interior was stark, with only a few pieces of tattered furniture. A small TV was tuned to the shopping channel, which was touting a line of luggage, perfect for the world traveler. The living room opened into the kitchen, which was stacked with dirty plates and empty liquor bottles, heavy with the smell of spoiled food. Linda sank into a threadbare recliner and sat watching the ice in her glass melt, not offering them a seat. Ella noticed only one photograph perched on the side table, an eight-by-ten picture of a younger Linda Ferron standing next to a beautiful bay horse.

"What a lovely animal," Ella said.

Linda's eyes came into focus. "That was Lancelot. He was the finest jumper I ever owned."

Ella tried to decide how to steer the conversation toward Bruce Reed, but Owen plunged in with the direct approach.

"Did you buy any horses on the advice of Bruce Reed?"

She blinked. "Oh, did I, but Lancelot I bought on my own. He was like the child I never had."

They both waited until Ella prodded her again. "Your sister said you knew Bruce Reed fairly well."

"Well enough. He was a charmer, wasn't he, that Bruce Reed? Knew everything about horses and treated me like a queen once he found out I had some money from my ex-husband to spend. Dinners, dancing, horse shows, and I opened up my checkbook, of course. First one horse, two, a trailer, and then, well, wouldn't you know, the horses turned out not to be worth what I paid, and the trailer was stolen before I had it insured. But just a little more money, one more investment and everything would be just fine. So a couple of thousand here and there and soon my problems weren't gone, but my money sure was."

"Did you go to the police?"

"Oh, there was no proof. My own stupid choices to purchase. Nobody's signature on the dotted line but mine. He would never be so foolish as to put his name on anything."

She felt a stab of desperation. There had to be something they could take to Larraby, one bit of hard evidence.

"There was only one way out to cover the debt." Linda's eyes filled with tears as she looked at

the picture of Lancelot. "He was such a beautiful horse."

Horror began to fill her. Ella took a breath.
"Lancelot was heavily insured?"

She nodded.

She had to force the words across her dry
mouth. "Did Bruce Reed arrange to have him
killed for the insurance payoff?"

"Such a beautiful animal and noble, gentle, but
the creditors you see…" Her haunted eyes roamed
the photo. "My car was repossessed, I lost my
house. I had nothing left, except for Lancelot."

Ella sighed and closed her eyes. Bruce Reed,
he was responsible for ruining Linda Ferron, and
once he'd gotten every last dime out of her, he'd
left her without a backward glance and moved on
to Candy Silverton.

"I'm so sorry," Ella said, throat thick.

"Oh, me too, honey," Linda croaked. "Sorry
I ever laid eyes on Bruce Reed." Her cell phone
rang. She fished it out of her pocket. Her expression went stark as she listened. After several hard
swallows, she disconnected without saying a word
to the caller. Ella and Owen exchanged a puzzled
glance.

With a shaking hand, Linda filled her glass
from a bottle of whiskey, gulping a swallow so
quickly it sloshed onto her shirt. "I'm a drunk,"
she said. "No one believes me and I guess they
shouldn't, really."

"You can get help," Ella said, moving closer and kneeling so Linda had to look her in the face. "It doesn't have to be like this."

"Spare me the fairy tale, honey," she said, mouth pinched. "There's winners and losers in life and I've lost. There's no getting it back. Bruce taught me that. He was raised poor as a church mouse, with a whole bunch of siblings, but he was small, like his mother, so he got picked on a lot. He said he learned early to point his nose toward the money and follow the trail until he got what he wanted. But I don't think it was all about the money. I think it was about the score. Pulling one over on people so he could feel smarter, bigger than they were. Bruce Reed needs to be the biggest man in the room, no matter what the cost." Her gaze drifted once more to the photo and tears gathered.

"Anyway, you know, I do have some photos and stuff, with Bruce and me together. And there's some old papers and checks and the like, if you want to look through them."

Ella straightened. "Really? That would be very helpful."

Owen's forehead creased in a frown, but Ella pressed on.

"May we look right now? I promise we won't make a mess."

"Might as well. I got no appointments to keep." She took one last drink from the glass and struggled from the chair, leading them outside behind the trailer. "In there," she said, pointing to a metal shed about fifteen feet high with a rusted metal roof. With Owen's help she shoved aside some stacks of newspaper and wrenched open the door. It gave with a shriek. The dark interior was stacked with moldy cardboard boxes, an old saddle and a desiccated bale of hay.

"It's a mess, but you can poke around to your heart's content. I'm not gonna help you, though."

"No problem," Ella said. "We'll just take a look and let you know when we're done, okay?"

She nodded, sucking on the tip of her index finger. "Make yourself at home."

Ella stepped inside, shuddering as a cobweb drifted along her cheek.

The dust filtered through the space, making her sneeze.

"God bless you," Owen said. "I'm…"

His comment was lost by the shed door being slammed shut. She and Owen both sprang for the opening, but Linda had slid something between the handles and locked them in.

Owen threw himself at the doors without hesitation, but the metal held in spite of the rust. He hammered with his fist. "Linda, let us out. Was it Bruce Reed who called you and told you to do this? You don't have to do what he says."

Ella was on her cell phone. "I called the police. I'm looking up the number for the trailer park office."

"Look fast," he said.

Her eyes went wide as Linda slid a burning piece of newspaper under the door. He stomped it out, but she followed with another and this time before he could douse the flame, it caught a stack of cardboard and flames began to devour the dried paper, pouring smoke into the cramped space.

"Get back and cover your mouth," he yelled, still trying to smother the flames. It was no use; the piles were the perfect kindling and the flames began to crawl from stack to stack. The temperature climbed rapidly and sweat poured down his temples.

Ella yelled into her phone. "Dory, help us. We're locked in a shed behind your sister's trailer. She trapped us in here and it's on fire."

He huffed out a breath, relieved that help was on its way until Ella said, "No one answered. I left a message."

The cops would be five minutes at least, and they'd be near dead of smoke inhalation by then. Ella grabbed his shoulder and pointed up. There was a small skylight set into the corrugated roof, almost obscured by the piles of junk. Immediately, he scrambled up a stack of wooden crates but the wood snapped like matchsticks under his weight and he crashed back down into a pile of papers.

Ella helped him up, coughing against the smoke that filled the shed. "Let me try."

She restacked the crates, discarding the broken ones and gingerly climbed up, but she was several feet shy of reaching the skylight.

"You've got to get on my shoulders," he called over the whoosh of the fire as it spread to a roll of brittle carpet.

"But…"

He didn't wait for her to elucidate. Injury or not, it was time for Owen to do his best ladder impression. He moved next to her, helping as much as he could while she climbed onto his back. Holding the wall for balance, she got one foot up on his shoulder and then another. Grinding his teeth together to keep from crying out, he grabbed her ankles and maneuvered underneath the skylight.

She pressed her palms to the dirty glass. "It's fastened in place and there's no way to open it," she yelled. The smoke was funneling upward, burying her in an acrid fog that set her choking.

"Air's too bad," he yelled. "You have to come down."

"One more try. Maybe I can break it," she rasped out. This time she pounded against the glass. He felt her feet tremble on his shoulders and he worked desperately to keep her from falling. The glass held fast and the smoke was now completely filling the apex. She tumbled and he tried to catch her. Together they fell into a pile of newspapers and plastic garbage bags.

"We can't get out," she said, cheeks filthy from the smoke, tears making streaks through the grime.

He pulled her into the shelter of his arms, turning her face to his chest. "Breathe against me."

Ella wasn't sure exactly how long it took for a person to die of smoke inhalation, but she figured they had to be getting close. Even with her mouth pressed to Owen's chest, her lungs burned from inhaling the noxious air.

She gripped his shirt. "I'm sorry," she said. *Sorry for dragging you into this. Sorry you are the kind of man who won't turn your back on your duty even if it gets you killed. Sorry I didn't realize how much you meant to me.*

"Don't be sorry." He pressed a kiss to her sweaty forehead and snuggled her closer. "Help's coming."

Would it get here in time? She didn't know, but she realized that she was enduring her worst moment with her best friend. Owen Thorn had been a part of her life every day, because even when he'd been gone she'd held him close to her heart. Curling her arms around him, she held him and she prayed, for their deliverance from the flames and for the lion-hearted Owen Thorn.

As they lay cocooned together, the heat rising

to unbearable levels, she thought she heard a shout from outside. Her senses dizzied, she struggled to move air in and out of her lungs. Owen lifted his head and yelled something she couldn't make out.

Her ears reverberated with the roar and crackle of the fire, which seemed to have spread everywhere, creeping closer and closer to their tiny refuge, filling every square inch with suffocating smoke. The walls shuddered around them and suddenly a rush of air fanned the flames even higher, and she believed she must surely be roasting alive. She was seized by her shoulders and dragged from the burning shed.

Owen, Owen, Owen. Was he behind? Had they gotten him out too?

Her rescuers multiplied as someone took her feet and another her shoulders and she was carried away from the heat. Blessedly cool air bathed her face as she was placed carefully on a patch of grass.

Where's Owen? she wanted to shout, but her mouth was parched dry and coated with bitter soot.

"Easy, honey," Dory said. "Get some water," she ordered a man in a delivery service uniform. "Look out, everyone," she called out. "Ambulance is coming."

Rolling onto her side she coughed violently, unable to stop until a palm cupped her chin. She forced her eyes open. Owen's face swam into view. He too was lying on his side next to her, eyes watering just as much as her own, blue as those long ago summer days when they were children and life stretched ahead of them like an endless adventure. Her brain was addled, body offline, but he was there with her.

"Don't leave me," she said, her own voice unrecognizable to her. "Please don't leave me."

He brushed the hair away from her cheek. "Shhhh," he said. "I'm right here and I'm not going anywhere, Ella Jo."

Her mind knew it was not a promise he could keep in the future, but for now, for this one moment she let herself believe it. An ambulance rolled up and she and Owen were placed on stretchers with oxygen masks over their mouths.

Dory appeared once more before the ambulance started for the hospital. "I'm so sorry. My sister took off. The police will find her. I can't... Well, I know she's done some bonehead stuff, but I didn't think she would ever do something like this."

Bruce Reed destroys people, Ella wanted to say, but she could only manage a nod before they were en route to the hospital. The paramedic took her vitals and talked soothingly. For some reason, Ella could not stop crying, tears rolling down her face, dampening the crisp white sheet they'd draped her with.

Owen reached out and took her hand in his. He didn't say a word and he didn't have to.

I'm here, his touch said. *And I'm not going anywhere.*

EIGHTEEN

Owen was pronounced hale enough after a few hours of oxygen, a chest X-ray and blood tests. His throat was raw, a sensation that did not diminish after he downed a glass of water. As he sat upright in the bed pulling on his filthy clothes, he replayed what Ella had said.

Don't leave me. Please don't leave me. He knew she must have been foggy, her thoughts askew from the smoke inhalation and too much carbon monoxide in her system, but the words would not retreat from his mind.

Don't leave me. He felt the tug of that request rumbling around his soul, the frightening pleasure of being needed so deeply by someone whom he cared about.

But he was going to do exactly that, just like he'd planned.

I'm made for war.

You're made for more than that.

It was the first time in his adult life when he'd

faltered, when he'd imagined a different path, when he'd heard a voice calling from another direction. *Don't leave me.* But that was a path that couldn't be taken. He was meant to return to the marines as soon as he brought down Bruce Reed.

But what if you didn't? There it was again, the whisper of a strange idea from far away. That thought stopped him, froze him in place. *What if you stayed?*

His brain supplied the answer. Then he would undoubtedly be as terrible a husband as Ray predicted.

He would always fear deep down that he hadn't been good enough to return to the marines.

He would disappoint Ella eventually, disappoint them both.

Friendship was all he could offer.

He asked the nurse about Ella's condition. "We're waiting on one more blood test," the nurse said, "but I think she'll be okay to be released in a couple of hours."

Thank you, God.

He played down the incident to his family when they called, told them not to come, explained that they were both fine and would be home soon. The local cop who'd already spoken to him earlier was just stepping outside Ella's room when he got there. "She's asleep right now, but I think I have enough details to move forward."

She'd obviously told him what they both believed.

Bruce Reed was behind it. He'd scared Linda Ferron into trapping them with some threat or another.

"Already spoke to Officer Larraby and filled him in," the cop said. "We'll continue to look for Linda Ferron and keep you updated on our progress."

Owen thanked him. After the officer departed, he sat in the chair next to Ella. She looked very small there in the bed, the fringe of her brilliant red hair singed and blackened. He reached over and fingered the burnt ends, anger swelling inside.

Bruce Reed will pay for every single strand, he promised.

His phone buzzed with a text. Why is there no answer from Ella at the house?

Ray. He considered his reply. Felt she and Betsy were safer at the ranch he texted back.

He imagined Ray reading his message, trying to make sense of it.

More threats?

He would not lie to his friend. Yes.

Do whatever you have to, man.

I will.

And don't let her get too comfortable there at the ranch.

He knew the truth behind what he imagined was supposed to be a kidding tone. Ray was right. Owen knew his faults; he was stubborn, prideful, a guy who could talk to horses easier than people, and was probably a fool more than he would ever admit, a man with anger, a man with a broken body.

Most of all, he was the kind of man that didn't stick around. Ella deserved a partner who would stay, one who was willing to make her priority number one. She'd been left behind enough, by him, by Ray, by her father.

Ella stirred and sighed. He moved closer and before he fully understood his own actions, he'd touched his mouth to hers, one gentle kiss that filled him with a profound sadness for what he knew he could not have.

Her eyes opened and he realized there was no color more beautiful in all God's creation than the soft green tint of Ella Cahill's eyes. She swam back to consciousness.

"How are you feeling?" he said.

She cleared her throat. "Like a horse kicked me in the head."

"That's the carbon monoxide. Doc said it will dissipate soon."

"I wonder what he considers *soon*." She rubbed her forehead. "Can I go home now?"

"Soon."

She frowned. "There's that word again. Have they caught Linda Ferron?"

"No, but they will…"

"If you say *soon* again I'll deck you."

He smiled at her sass. "I was going to say 'keep us posted.'"

"Oh, right." She bit her lip. "I feel sorry for Linda."

He raised an eyebrow. "Linda almost killed us."

"I know, but Bruce ruined her financially and emotionally. I'm worried if we don't stop him he'll do the same to Candy. He's already cost her her nephew and she still won't believe anything bad about Reed."

"The cops will find Linda." He refrained from adding *soon*. "In the meantime, we can see how Team Thorn is doing tracking down Reed's wife. Maybe she will be more helpful."

"Right." Her phone buzzed and he handed it to her. Her frown deepened as she read the message. "It's my lawyer. I have to schedule a meeting to go over my defense, if I can think of one." She looked so burdened with worry that he reached over and tousled her hair.

"Hey, kiddo. We're going to find evidence to clear you. We're getting close."

"We were close with the thermos and then with Linda. One step forward, one colossal leap backward."

"That's not the attitude that wins battles."

"It's hard to be positive when my head is pounding and I smell like a barbecue."

"I wasn't going to bring it up, but you do kinda smell a little on the well-done side."

"Come closer so I can deck you now." She quirked a pained smile and his soul rejoiced while at the same time his gut quivered with worry. She was right—they hadn't turned up anything to incriminate Bruce Reed, but they'd nearly been killed. That had to indicate they were getting close, didn't it?

It was as if he could hear the moments ticking down on the clock, closer and closer. To victory? Or to her imprisonment?

Speed it up, Owen. You're running out of time.

Ella insisted that Owen stop at a thrift store before they drove back to Gold Bar. "I am not spending one more moment in smoky clothes and neither are you."

"You go ahead. It's only an hour drive," he said. "I can wait."

"With you driving, it's more like two."

He ignored the jibe. "I don't like clothes shopping. I'm very hard to please."

"Then I'll pick for you." She opened the passenger door and he tried to hand her some money.

Her face went red and he realized he'd hurt her pride. "I can afford some used clothing, Owen." Slamming the door behind her, she strode into the thrift shop, head high.

How would she feel about the order he'd placed just before they left to meet Linda for Betsy's new wheelchair cushion? It was a battle for another day. In fifteen minutes, she returned with a large paper sack and they stopped at a café, ordered coffee to go and she used the bathroom to change. She emerged with baggy sweatpants and a long-sleeved green knit shirt that made her eyes sparkle like gems. She held out a shirt to him.

He clutched the shirt. "I can't wear this," he said, holding up the garment emblazoned with a white cartoonish unicorn. The I Break for Unicorns shirt was at least in a manly gray color.

She began to giggle, eventually laughing so hard she almost dropped the bag. "I think it suits you, and besides, it was the only thing big enough to fit."

"I can't…"

"Change," she ordered. "I'll wait for you in the parking lot."

"But…"

"Tick tock, Owen."

Grumbling, he took the clothes and found the restroom. She'd done all right with the jeans, though they were not the style he preferred and would be transferred to the bottom of the closet the moment he got home. When he rejoined her, she started laughing all over again.

"I'm putting my own shirt back on," he said, turning.

She grabbed his wrist. "No way. I finally got the smoke out of my lungs, Owen. Don't mess up the air in the car again."

"If anybody sees me in this, my life is over."

"You can tell them you're in disguise."

"Disguises are meant for you to blend in. No one wears disguises with unicorns on them."

"Trendsetter," she teased.

On impulse he ducked behind the truck, emerging a few seconds later with a triumphant grin and the shirt worn inside out. "There."

"Now you look like you can't dress yourself."

"Better than people thinking I wear unicorn shirts." Muttering, he got into the truck and accepted the cup of coffee. She handed over a foil-wrapped hot dog. "There was a stand next to the thrift store. Here's one with your favorite condiment," she said. "Maybe it will make up for the shirt."

The hot dog was just the way he liked, plain except for one narrow ribbon of mustard, perfectly applied. It didn't quite negate the unicorn shirt, but his stomach appreciated the effort. She only ate half of her own hot dog, slathered with ketchup and sweet relish.

"Not hungry?"

She shook her head. "I guess it's all catching up with me. I just want to be home in time to watch *Jeopardy!* with Betsy and put this awful day behind me."

"Don't worry. Even with my snail-pace driving, as you put it, we'll be home in plenty of time."

A light rain spattered on the front windshield as predicted by the hourly Doppler he'd checked before they took off. The wipers kept time to his thoughts. If the cops found Linda Ferron, would her word be enough to implicate Bruce Reed? What about Reed's wife? How could the man with such a pattern of evil be so hard to pin with a crime? He was careful to cover his tracks, Owen had to give him that.

He thought Ella had drifted off to sleep, until she squirmed and fished for her phone.

"Hello?" Her mouth dropped open in surprise as she hit the speaker button. "Where are you?"

He heard sniffling, the sound of traffic.

"I'm scared," Linda said.

Then it was his turn to gape in surprise. Linda was on the phone? Took him a minute to remember Ella had given her a business card.

"Where are you?" Ella repeated. "We'll come and get you."

"He'll find me. I didn't want to lock you in the

shed, but he was watching, he knew I talked to you." More crying. "I'm scared, I'm scared. He'll kill me." Linda's voice rose to a wail.

"We won't let him hurt you. Tell us where you are and we'll send the police. They'll keep you safe."

There was a long pause. "I told the truth. I know I did bad things, terrible things, but in the end I told the truth, didn't I?"

"You're not making sense, Linda. Just take a breath. It's going to be okay. Tell me where you are, please."

"A coffee shop on Route Five, The Morning Joe."

Owen frantically punched in a search on his phone to locate the shop. "Ten minutes," he whispered to Ella.

"We'll be there in ten minutes," Ella said. "Linda, you go back inside and stay there. Nothing bad will happen, okay? Stay inside, do you hear me?"

With a sob, Linda disconnected.

Ella stared at him. "I'll call the police."

"And I'll head for Route Five." Ten minutes. As he pressed the accelerator, the clock began ticking down.

Ella sat on the edge of her seat. Linda was clearly distraught, and if Ella didn't know the police were on the way, she might have suspected the woman of luring them into another trap on behalf of Bruce Reed. But there had been something so pleading in Linda's voice, so desperate to be forgiven.

You are forgiven, as far as I'm concerned, Linda, just like I am. Uncharacteristically, Owen was driving at a good clip, and he covered the distance quickly.

"You're not getting out of this truck until the cops arrive," he said. "This could be another trap."

"I'm aware, Owen, so you don't need to go into commander mode."

"Okay," he said, slowing as they approached the main drag.

She craned her neck. "Did you hear a siren?"

"Yeah, coming from up the street a few blocks."

"Good." She huffed out a breath. "The police got there first."

He almost didn't want to say it. "Ella, that's an ambulance siren."

She pressed her hand to her mouth, fear clawing at her throat. "No, no," she breathed.

The road ahead was blocked by the ambulance. As they stopped at a light, a police car shot by them, coming to a stop ahead. Owen found a spot on the curb a block away from the café and turned to talk to Ella but she was already leaping out.

"Wait," he said, but he could not prevent her from running toward the coffee shop.

He had a terrible feeling that he knew what she was going to find when she got there.

NINETEEN

Ella's overworked lungs screamed in protest, but she ran anyway, coming to a hard stop next to the paramedic. She fell to her knees. Linda was lying on her back, eyes open only the tiniest slit, blood on the corner of her mouth, her breathing labored.

"It's okay, Linda," Ella said. "I'm here."

Linda's glasses were broken, lying shattered on the cement. Ella gently touched her forehead. "We'll get you to a hospital and you'll be okay."

Linda's lips moved and Ella bent closer to hear.

"Tell her…" she whispered.

"Tell who?"

"Tell my sister. Tell her I told the truth."

Ella could barely see through her tears. "I will tell her and she'll forgive you. God forgives you for everything, all of it."

Linda sighed and the crease eased from between her brows. "I told the truth." Her voice was no bigger than a murmur, and then her eyes closed.

"Linda…" Ella whispered, but there was no answer.

The medic gently steered Ella aside and she found herself in the circle of Owen's arms.

"I'm so sorry, Ella Jo."

She could not answer.

Another medic joined him and they worked on Linda for what seemed like a lifetime before they stepped back and covered her with a blanket.

Her brain refused to believe it. Linda could not be dead, not another victim like Luke. Her knees might have buckled were it not for Owen's arm supporting her.

The medic stood. "So you know this woman?"

Ella tried to speak but nothing would come out.

"Her name is Linda Ferron," Owen said. "She lives in a trailer park in Rock Ridge. What happened?"

"Witnesses said she took a phone call, ran out the front door and was struck by a vehicle. Hit-and-run. Driver didn't even stop."

Her stomach convulsed. "What type of car?" she whispered.

"Older model SUV."

Tony's vehicle.

A police officer drew them both aside. It was the same one who had interviewed them in the hospital.

"I can tell you what happened," Ella said, anger lending her the strength to string the words together. "She got a call from Bruce Reed or from his thug, Tony. Tony was waiting and he ran her down."

"How would he know where to find her?"

"My guess is Reed figured we'd be going to talk to Linda Ferron and he had Tony watching her. Tony reported we were there and Bruce called to order her to lock us in the shed. He probably followed her to the café. Tying up loose ends," Owen said bitterly.

"We'll analyze her phone calls," the officer said.

Ella didn't bother to reply. Reed wouldn't have used a traceable phone and neither would Tony. What's more, Reed no doubt had an ironclad alibi at the time the first phone call was made and the moment when Linda Ferron was run down. "Did anyone get a license plate number from the hit-and-run driver?"

"No. Witnesses said the rear plates were smeared with mud."

They followed the officer back to the station to file their formal statements and finally, in the late afternoon, they were on the road home. It was a silent drive. She could feel Owen sneaking glances at her but she closed her eyes and leaned against the cold window glass. What could she say? Reed had won again and finally completed his destruction of Linda Ferron. How much longer would it be before he destroyed her too?

* * *

With just a look, Owen told his family that it was not the right time to ask Ella any questions. He helped her move Betsy to Grandad's cabin and got them settled in.

Betsy caught his hand while Ella went to clean up. He wasn't sure how successful she'd be in washing away the terrible death of Linda Ferron. He knelt next to Betsy and though she didn't speak, he saw the question in her eyes.

"Your sister had a bad day today." He smoothed his palm over her fingers. "But she's going to be okay."

Her mouth crimped, but whether it was in worry or sadness for Ella, he did not know. He tightened his grasp on her fingers for a moment. "Betsy, I'm going to help Ella, me and my family. We're going to take care of her and you. Do you understand?"

She nodded and sent him a tender smile. He saw the Bible tucked under her elbow, a children's version, and he swallowed hard. "Do you…do you want me to read to you for a while?"

Again a nod, accompanied by an even bigger smile. She offered the book and it fell open to a well-worn story, Joseph and his amazing coat, which seemed to fascinate her.

When he finished, Ella was standing there in clean clothes, staring at them. He felt the weight of her emotion, but he wasn't sure how to respond. With more assurances that he would protect her, when she'd seen Linda Ferron die before her eyes? With another promise that he would not leave her, when he had every intention of doing exactly that?

"Uh, feel better?" Dumb thing to say, but she gave a tiny nod.

When the silence grew painful, he awkwardly filled it again. "I'll bring you two dinner in a while if you'd rather not eat in the kitchen, okay? I mean, of course, you're invited to eat with us, you know that."

Tears gleamed in her eyes. "Thank you." Her voice shook.

He fought the urge to kick something as he returned to his family and explained what had happened. His mother's face went slack with shock. "This is terrible. He's a monster."

"Have you found any info on his wife?"

She shook her head. "I'm sorry. I searched all day and Keegan joined in when he was done with the horses, but we can't find hide nor hair of her."

Nerves tightened throughout his body. There had to be something, some way to bring Reed down. He shoved the chair back and grabbed his jacket from the coatrack.

"Where are you going?" his mother called.

He could hear the fear in her voice.

"To find Reed." He tuned out the clamor of the dissenting voices behind him. Ripping open the door, he pounded down the front steps. By the time he got to the truck, Jack was there, climbing in the passenger side.

He gunned the engine, turning to his brother. "You here to try and talk me out of it?"

"No."

"Then what?"

"To watch your back."

Owen swallowed his answer. Even through the shimmering haze of rage, he was grateful to have his brother beside him. No matter how much he sinned, how far he'd wandered, Jack and Keegan and Barrett would always support him. He silently thanked God as he lead-footed the accelerator. Heading straight for Candy Silverton's property, he wasted no time banging on the door.

Candy opened, wrapped in a blue terry robe. "What are you doing here?" Her eyes widened in surprised as she got a gander at his singed hair. "What happened to you? You smell like you've been in a fire."

"Where's Reed?"

"Why do you want to know?"

"Because he had a woman killed today. You're probably not going to believe me, but it's the truth. Ella and I almost died too. I want to talk to Reed. Now."

Her startled gaze shifted from him to Jack and back again. Then she stepped aside. "Come in." She gestured for them to take a seat in the sleek leather armchairs, but they remained standing. Scattered along the glass-topped coffee table were pictures of her nephew Luke.

"I'm trying to plan his memorial," she said, a wobble in her voice.

Owen blew out a breath. Candy was a victim of Reed also, whether she knew it or not. She didn't deserve Owen's hostility. "Where is he, Miss Silverton?" he asked in a gentler tone.

"He's away checking on my broodmares."

Owen ground his teeth in frustration.

"Tell me what happened to you," Candy said.

Owen did, omitting no details, including the hit-and-run death of Linda Ferron.

Candy bit her lip. "He told me he'd tried to help Linda in the past, but she was a raging alcoholic and she was beyond help."

"Because he made her that way."

She listened, tapping a fingernail against her lip. "It's all so crazy, these allegations."

"Has Tony turned up?"

"No. The police told me they would let me know as soon as they caught him."

"I told you he drove us off the bridge."

The worried crimp of her brow made him think she at least believed him about that.

"How did Tony come to work here?"

She hesitated. "Bruce hired him. They worked together before at some stable or another, but that doesn't prove anything. He didn't know Tony was a criminal. Maybe Tony killed Luke and framed Ella for it."

Progress. At least Candy was ready to consider the possibility that Ella was innocent. "Or maybe Reed is trying to scam you out of your money, like he did with Linda Ferron and probably others."

She jerked as if he'd slapped her, walking to the wide bank of windows that looked out over her acres of moonlit pastures. "I don't want to believe that. You're grasping at straws to keep Ella out of prison."

He fought for calm. "Miss Silverton, I saw a woman die today, a woman whose life was wrecked by Bruce Reed. I don't want to see that happen again, not to Ella and not to you."

He waited, breath held.

Still with her back to him, she opened the small drawer of the secretary desk. Turning, she handed him a piece of paper.

"What is this?"

"I... I snooped in Bruce's wallet after I visited you in the hospital. I found this phone number. I had a friend search the name."

Owen held his breath.

"Who does it belong to?" Jack asked.

"His wife, Violet Wilder."

She pressed the paper in his hand and his thoughts whirled. The next lead, another move toward bringing Reed down. "And you're giving me this information? Does that mean you believe me about Reed?"

She snuggled the robe around her tighter. "I'm not really giving you anything, I just want you to know I'm not an idiot. People always think your life is easy if you're rich, and I guess it is in a way, but it comes at a cost. All my life I've been surrounded by people who butter up to me because I'm an heiress. Everyone from the town vet to the grocery store guy. I've had some relationships in my life and they've all turned out to be a series of people looking to get a piece of the Silverton pie. That hurts, you know?"

A sheen of moisture glimmered in her eyes. He'd never considered how difficult it must be to approach every relationship with suspicion, walls up, one foot out the door. "I guess it would."

"And Bruce is the first one in a very long time to make me feel like I'm worthy to be loved, fortune or no fortune."

He clamped his lips together to keep from saying, *Reed is the worst of the lot.*

"To be honest, I don't want to lose that. I've come to love Bruce and that was not easy for me." She looked suddenly tired, the lines around her lips pronounced. "So I'm not ready to take your word for it about him."

"But…"

She held up a palm. "But I'm saying I will be

cautious and check some things out. First off, I want to know why he didn't tell me he had a wife."

Owen gripped the paper. "We'll look into it, tell you anything we come up with after we talk to her."

"You won't be doing that."

"What do you mean?"

"Violet Wilder died fifteen years ago in a train derailment."

TWENTY

Just before bedtime, Ella opened the door to Zeke Potter and invited him to sit with her in Grandad's front room. Betsy waved from her spot at the table where she was putting together a simple puzzle.

"Came to check on you," he said. "Sorry it's so late. Mrs. Thorn said it was okay."

She curled up with her feet underneath her, hair still wet from her earlier shower.

"You look half in," he said, after a pause. "You okay?"

She swallowed hard against the tears that threatened and told him in low tones the gist of what had happened. He leaned back against the sofa cushions and passed trembling fingers over his forehead. "I can't fathom it."

They sat in silence for a while. Ella noticed Zeke looked thinner, careworn. "What's the matter, Zeke?"

He squirmed. "Hardly seems right to tell you in light of your own troubles."

"Tell me anyway."

"I, uh, wanted to let you know that I'm retiring."

"What? Why?"

"Just the expense of it all. Can't keep up with the bills. Gonna have to sell my place."

His home had been in his family for three generations. Tears crowded her lids. "I wish… I wish I had some money I could loan you. You've been so good to me."

His face reddened. "Ain't that just like you? To want to help me even though you're in a heap of trouble yourself?"

"You helped me when I hit rock bottom and I'll never forget that."

"You don't owe me anything, not one thing. Anyway, it's my own fault. Dumb guy like me ought not to be tossing money away on the ponies."

Gambling. His vice. She thought he'd given it up for good, prayed for it. "How bad?"

"Awww, I owed some people, bad people, but it's paid off now. Paid with my soul, Ella. There's nothing left."

She took his wrists. "You can start again. I'll help you, when… I mean, after the trial." But they both knew where she might be living after the trial. The clang of the cell door roared in her ears.

"It's okay, Ella. This old bear will be all right.

I'm gonna stay on for a few months until I can get the house sold, but I wanted to give you this…"

It was his hammer, the one from his father who had been a farrier until the day he died.

She touched the hickory handle, which had been shaped to fit his father's hand, then Zeke's. "I can't accept it. It's too much."

"It's the only thing I got to give you. I feel so bad about all your trouble, Ella. If there was some way I could undo what's happened…"

"The only way is to stop Bruce Reed."

He grew serious. "It just doesn't seem possible."

She jutted her chin. "I will find a way. I have to. Betsy and I won't ever be safe until he's in prison."

He folded her palm around the hammer, enveloping her hand in his calloused grip. "Be careful, Ella."

"I will be."

He shuffled down the path, shoulders hunched against the vast Gold Country sky. How many people over the centuries had come to this part of the world, hoping to find their fortunes, only to lose everything? The thought of Zeke throwing away his life for that feverish hope that the next wager would be his salvation crushed her. She said a prayer then and there that somehow, some way, God would save Zeke from the destruction he'd wrought. It felt like the final blow to have him walk out of her life. Her father, Ray, Owen…

She blinked hard and picked up the hammer,

smoothing her fingers over the worn handle. Outside the horses nickered, silhouetted in the molten rays of the setting sun. Would she ever be able to return to her farrier work? If not, how would she provide for Betsy?

Cart before the horse, she told herself sternly. *If you don't find a way to beat Bruce Reed, nothing else matters.*

Linda Ferron's pleading face swam before her eyes.

Tell my sister.

It was one thing she knew she must do.

"I'll tell her," Ella whispered to herself. "I promise."

Owen did not see much of Ella and Betsy on Saturday, and Ella refused to go to the morning church service on Sunday.

"I'll attend the evening one with Betsy," she said.

He understood why—less people to stare, to whisper. It infuriated him, left him tossing and turning that night until Monday morning finally arrived and he could throw himself into his chores. A predawn ride with Glory soothed his jangled nerves but did not provide him any insight on how to proceed with his assault on Bruce Reed's Teflon reputation. His phone reminded him of his physical therapy appointment and he went with a hitch in his gut.

What if the doctor said he could not recover? That his marine career really was over and done with? Though he felt like pacing, he forced himself to remain still in the hardbacked waiting room chair until it was time. The doctor did her usual torturous range of motion tests and then she sat back in the seat and gestured him into another.

"You continue to progress, Owen. Running a ranch is better than any exercises I could prescribe. So what do you want from me?"

"I want you to give me the green light to return to my unit."

She cocked her head. "Is that still what you want?"

"Yes, ma'am. Why would you question it?"

She tapped a pen on her desk. "I've known you and your family a long time, Owen. Since you were that high school football player with the beat-up ankle who could not stomach the thought of missing a game."

He nodded for her to continue.

"You've beaten back so much adversity here in the States," she said. "Overcome your pain-killer addiction, worked to reacclimatize yourself to peacetime." She shrugged. "I know you're helping Ella Cahill through her ordeal."

He laughed. "Small towns. News travels, huh?"

"Well, that was pretty big news, her being accused of murder."

"We're gonna prove her innocent."

"Before you reenlist?"

He folded his arms. "Okay. What are you really getting at, doc?"

"I feel like I can say this to you because I've known you for so long. There's a calm to you that I've not seen before, and it makes me wonder if you've found what you needed here at home."

Confusion rifled through him. Calm? He hadn't noticed that the coiled spring of tension inside him had loosened a bit of late. Why? Did it matter? He was a marine, born to do it, destined for it, made for war. That had not changed. It was his dream and always would be until he was ready for his pine box.

"I need to re-up."

"Why?"

He bristled. "Because it's my dream and you're supposed to be consulting on my leg, not my life."

She looked away.

He blew out a breath. "I'm sorry. I apologize. I was rude."

"So was I, I guess. You're right. You came to me about the leg, so that's what I'll report on. Here's the straight answer. You will probably never regain full range of motion in that leg. There was just too much damage to the musculature. You will likely always limp and have to live with chronic pain for the rest of your life."

His heart plummeted.

"However, in my opinion, you have recovered sufficiently enough to do your job as a marine. Congratulations, Owen."

He laughed as his lungs resumed their rhythm and her pronouncement awakened excitement he had not felt in a long while. "You almost had me scared there for a minute."

"I thought marines were never scared."

"That's why I said *almost.*"

They shook hands and he thanked her again. On his way back to the truck, he puzzled over her comments. It was true he had left the ferocious painkiller cravings behind, and the wild nights of pacing like a caged lion had passed.

…it makes me wonder if you've found what you needed here at home.

No, he decided. His dream had not changed. He wanted more than anything, with every fiber and pulse, to return to his unit, and that's what he would do. With a light heart, he walked through the front lobby where he found the receptionist standing on the front step, peering up the street.

"What's going on?"

"I don't know, but a cop car just pulled up at the Sunrise Café."

He followed her gaze. A crowd of people collected on the sidewalk outside the establishment. Stomach plummeting, he recognized his brother Keegan's motorcycle parked on the sidewalk, just ahead of Larraby's squad car.

He sprinted toward the melee, shouldering aside the gawkers until he found his brother Keegan being restrained by Oscar Livingston, the manager of the Gold Nugget Inn.

"It's okay, son," Oscar said. "Get yourself under control."

Keegan was panting, nostrils flared, fury radiating from every fiber.

Bruce Reed faced him, a trickle of blood on the corner of his mouth. Larraby stood between them.

He went to his brother. "What happened?"

"He was spouting off," Keegan snarled. "Telling everyone how sad it was that Betsy would be alone once Ella went to prison. I told him to knock it off, but he wouldn't, so I shoved him and he banged his mouth."

"He would have seriously injured me if these people hadn't intervened," Reed said, swiping at his jaw.

"Yeah, I would have because you don't even know how to make a fist," Keegan said.

"Knock it off, Keegan," Larraby said.

"Just a shove is all," Oscar said. "No punches were thrown."

Keegan glared. "As if he could take a punch."

Owen pushed against Keegan's heaving chest. "Let it go."

"Uh-uh. Why should he be able to shoot his mouth off with lies about Ella?"

"Because this is America and he's allowed to say anything he wants," Larraby said. "Which means if he presses charges, you're going to jail, Keegan."

Larraby's eyes glittered greedily. Owen knew it was exactly what Larraby longed for.

"Do what you have to do, man," Keegan said. Owen pressed against Keegan's chest, felt the pulse of his brother's rage there. He knew that kind of anger because he'd felt it, lost control of it so many times.

"How's that justice, Owen?" Keegan snarled. "He gets to spread lies, ruin her reputation."

"It's not justice, Keeg. Justice doesn't live here, I've heard it said."

"Then what's wrong with this picture?" Keegan's eyes blazed at him. "You go overseas to bleed and take bullets and you come back home to this kind of enemy?" He jutted his chin at Reed. "How can you take it?"

"Because you have to and because you have other people who need you." Owen heard his brother Jack's wisdom coming out of his mouth and it surprised him. When had the switch flipped in his mind? The moment he considered that however much he detested Bruce Reed, he loved his brother more. And right now, Keegan needed someone to hold the reins steady.

Owen turned to Reed. "So are you pressing charges or not?"

Reed considered, his sly glance taking in the crowd gathered around. "No," he said finally. "I'll overlook it this time."

Owen faced him head-on. "Don't think you're

gonna get a thank-you from us," Owen said, "because my brother is right. Ella Cahill is innocent and the filth you're spreading won't stop the truth from coming out about you."

He nodded a thank-you to Oscar, turned Keegan around and marched him back to his bike. His brother was still breathing hard, jaw set.

Owen gestured. "Go home. I'll follow."

"It's not right."

"I know, so let's go home and figure out how to win."

Keegan didn't reply. He pulled away from the curb and took off.

Reed's smile sliced into Owen as he left.

He wondered at the crowd milling around Reed, one offering him a handkerchief to dab at the blood on his mouth. Some of them had lived in Gold Bar for generations. He knew Oscar supported Ella. He figured Peg did too, from the wave she gave him as he got into his truck. But as for the rest, would they believe in Ella's innocence?

Or had she already been found guilty in their hearts?

Didn't matter, he told himself savagely. He'd find enough evidence that they'd have to.

Justice may not live in Gold Bar, but he would make sure it was a captive visitor until Ella was cleared once and for all.

TWENTY-ONE

Ella knew something was up when she got off the old kitchen phone with Dory. Keegan threw himself down in a chair, looking murderous. Owen's mouth was pinched into a grim line. Neither one was going to talk about it in spite of Mrs. Thorn's badgering.

"Nothing," Owen said. "Just a misunderstanding at the café with Reed."

Ella's stomach constricted. "What kind of misunderstanding?"

"Reed was slandering Ella and he needed someone to shut his mouth for him," Keegan said.

Mrs. Thorn groaned.

"It's okay," Owen said. "It's over. No harm done."

But Ella knew there had been plenty of harm done, probably to her reputation, and now to Keegan's. "Oh, Keegan. Please don't get tangled up with Reed on my behalf. Bad enough that Owen's been his target."

"I can handle Reed," Keegan snapped.

"But you won't," Evie said. "That's not going to solve anything and it's going to land you in jail. Do you really want to give your half brother a chance to throw you in a cell?"

Keegan didn't answer. The room sank into an uncomfortable silence.

Ella bit her lip. A gathering darkness seemed to be enveloping her, spreading to everyone who tried to help her. Betsy, Linda Ferron, Owen, now Keegan.

Evie let out a breath, straightened her shoulders and turned to her older son. "Anyway, how did your doctor appointment go with Dr. Von, honey?"

Owen lifted an eyebrow. "How did you know I went to the doctor?"

"I told you, it's the detective in me."

He chuckled. "As a matter of fact, it went great. I'm cleared to go back to my unit."

Ella knew it was coming, knew that it was Owen's heart's desire to reenlist, but hearing the words pulled the shadows even closer, chilling her inside. She tried to picture it…the Gold Bar Ranch with three brothers instead of four.

Ella Cahill without Owen Thorn.

Evie offered a bright smile. "Well, I know that's your dream, so I am happy you got the news you wanted to hear."

He pressed a kiss to her temple. "And I know it's news that causes you pain, Mama. I'm sorry."

"I'll admit it's been a joy to have you home, but I've prayed you through all the tough times in your life and I will keep on praying even harder, especially if you're off to Afghanistan again."

Ella felt Owen looking at her, so she composed her face into something resembling a pleased expression. "That's great, Owen. All that killer physical therapy paid off."

"Thanks, but I want you to know I'm not going anywhere until your case is settled."

Until his duty to her was done. Why did the notion pain her so?

Because you love him.

There it was, the truth that she could not ignore. She loved him, deeply, desperately, fully… and futilely.

She was his childhood friend, nothing more. A duty to be completed and left behind. *The story of her life.* When he'd promised not to leave her in that hospital room, it was never meant to be permanent—she knew that. But how had she let it escape her thoughts for one minute?

"I'll be fine. I'm going to go check on Betsy. She was extra tired and she needed a late morning nap." The urgency to flee from that room bit into her and she hurtled toward the front door.

"Hold on," Owen said, catching up to her on the porch. "I've got something for you, for Betsy, I mean."

He handed over a bulky plastic-wrapped object, but she recognized it at once—the new wheelchair cushion that Betsy so desperately needed. Her cheeks heated as she stared at it. "I can't afford it."

"It's a gift, from a friend."

From a friend.

"It's too generous. We can't accept it." She tried to hand it back to him, but he would not take it.

"Sure you can."

"Owen, we're not a charity case."

"I don't see you like that."

The floodgates opened. "No, you just see me as your best friend's kid sister who needs a protector and someone to fix all her problems. Well, I don't, okay? I've taken care of Betsy all my life and I don't need you to start in now and make us need you and then take off on the next plane like Ray does."

His mouth opened in surprise. "What kind of talk is that?"

"The truth." Something spurred her to spew out the rest, tossed like grenades into the winter air. "Thank you for what you've done, but don't help anymore. I'm tired of being your mission, so you can feel good about yourself and make Ray proud."

Now he was out-and-out staring. "You're being unreasonable. Stress has gotten to you."

"No, it hasn't, Owen."

His mouth crimped. "Is that really how you feel?"

"Yes, it is." Her heart thumped hard against her ribs. *No, it's not. I love you.* Thoughts that mercifully stayed in her mind.

He looked at his boots, a vein jumping in his jaw, and she knew she'd wounded him, angered him perhaps, but at that moment, she was glad of it because he was leaving and because she loved the stubborn marine cowboy who did not love her back.

"Here," she said, thrusting the cushion back at him. "Maybe you can return it."

He stared at her then, blue eyes hard as a frozen lake. "Don't let your pride get in the way of what your sister needs."

"Don't you dare tell me how to take care of my sister."

"Your sister needs this cushion, so hang on to that chip on your shoulder if you want to, but take it for her sake." He turned on his heel and strode off toward the corral.

Stomach churning, she stomped back to the cabin. Chip on her shoulder? She tossed the cushion on the sofa. Pride? No, she thought, more like hurt and anger. That's what was keeping her from taking the precious gift that would ease her sister's pain.

Curling up on the sofa, she clutched the cushion and cried.

* * *

Owen forked out the afternoon flakes of hay until the sweat ran down his temples.

I'm tired of being your mission, so you can feel good about yourself and make Ray proud. He was still reeling. All he'd done was bought a lousy cushion and nearly gotten his head lopped off for it. And what was she talking about, her being his mission? He didn't understand what he felt about Ella, but it was definitely not obligation. No, it was something entirely different that turned his brain to mush and made his fingers want to reach out for her every single moment.

Had he made her feel she was his duty because he was a bull in a china shop kinda guy about relationships? Action instead of emotion? Service in place of sentimentality? The kind of guy who had never bought a sappy greeting card and would rather clean out stalls than watch lovey-dovey romantic movies? But what kind of relationship did he want with Ella anyway? The freckle-faced kid was gone and a beautiful woman had taken her place, a woman who cantered through his thoughts like a spirited filly.

But like it or not she did need taking care of, and he wasn't about to let her own mile-wide stubborn streak open her up to attack. When he saw her wheel Betsy into the house, a small pack slung across her back, he waited. She was going somewhere and he was going to find out where, one way or the other.

She emerged a short while later as he leaned against the whitewashed fence, arms crossed.

"Going somewhere?"

She blushed crimson. "Just running an errand."

"Want company?"

Not from you, her look said loud and clear. "No, thank you. I can handle it."

"I don't think…"

"I said I can handle it," she snapped before blowing out a breath. "Owen, I apologize. I was rude before. It was very generous of you to buy that cushion for Betsy. She was grateful to have it and I appreciate your gesture, but I am going to pay you back for it when I can."

"Not necessary."

"Yes, it is." Her eyes pleaded with him to understand. "I have to take care of things by myself. It doesn't pay to rely on other people."

Who aren't going to stick around. The thought stung.

"I get it, Ella," he said softly. "But I'm here and the horses are fed, so I might as well go with you on your errand. You're going to see Dory, aren't you?"

Her quick jerk told her he'd guessed right.

"Yes."

"Then I'm going with you."

She crossed her arms to match his. "I don't want you to."

"I don't care."

"I'm not doing anything dangerous."

He ignored her and got into the driver's side of Zeke Potter's loaner truck. "Your driving is dangerous enough, Ella Jo."

He probably shouldn't have tossed her nickname in there. He sat there, waiting. It was possible he'd pushed too far, she'd storm back into the cabin and cancel her visit to Dory altogether, but he didn't think so. She'd promised she'd make things right between Linda and her sister, and that promise would outweigh the awkward inconvenience of a smart-aleck cowboy chaperone.

He was relieved when she yanked open the door and slid behind the wheel.

"You should bring a slicker. It's gonna rain," he said.

"There's not a cloud in the sky."

"I've been watching the Doppler. System moving down from Alaska in our direction. There's an eighty percent chance by four o'clock."

"You know there are other stations on the TV besides The Weather Channel? And other apps on your phone to choose for entertainment?"

"That right?" He eased back on the seat and perched his cowboy hat on his knee. "Did you know the place with the highest annual rainfall is Mahalaya, India? They get 467 inches, mostly during monsoon season."

"How do you have room in your brain for important things when you've got it all cluttered up with useless weather trivia?"

He tapped his temple. "Massive cranial capacity."

She didn't laugh, but he thought he caught the hint of a smile. At least her anger had ebbed to the point where he'd weaseled his way along. Point in his favor. If she meant to keep him at arm's length, he'd take whatever means necessary to protect her.

TWENTY-TWO

Ella drove like she always did, which was enough to make Owen gasp a few times at her lane changes. At one point, she noticed him clutching his cowboy hat, a pained look on his face.

Served him right for forcing himself into her outing, when she'd already told him she had to figure out her problems on her own. The meeting with her lawyer was four days away, and with each passing hour her conviction that she would find evidence to clear herself slipped into uncertainty.

But if she told her lawyer everything she knew about Bruce Reed, perhaps he could enlist an investigator to help, one that would be beyond the threats of Reed.

She recalled the picture Reed had texted of Betsy, scared and confused. It made her blood freeze. *So easy.*

But how would she protect Betsy without the Thorns' help?

It's just until the trial, she thought, swallowing the lump of fear in her throat. Then her fate would be sealed one way or the other.

Who will take care of Betsy if you go to prison? The thought burned inside her. She could not be a permanent guest at the ranch. Would Ray come home and take over her care?

Not likely. She didn't think he'd give up the marines for anything. She fought back a surge of resentment. Ray would help as best he could. She decided to call him and tell him everything. There had to be some solution if they put their heads together. Owen tensed in the seat next to her.

"What?"

"I thought I saw a dark SUV behind us. Maybe I'm being paranoid, but just in case how about we pull over at the next gas station. Don't kill the engine, okay?"

She nodded and did as he directed. They stared out the window, watching all the cars drive past them on the main road, her heart pounding like a jackhammer. There was no dark SUV among them. Had the driver pulled off, or maybe passed without his knowing it? Reed following them? Tony?

Owen offered a calm nod. "Nothing. Guess I was wrong."

His gaze remained riveted to the rear and side-view mirrors as they drove to the trailer park.

When they got there, Dory ushered them into

the office and settled them onto a small love seat that meant there was no place for Owen's arms to find a resting place except when he slung one around Ella's shoulders. She tried not to inhale the enticing smell of hay and horses and soap that was so much a part of him. The high trailer window was cracked, which allowed a wisp of chill air to creep in, probably in an effort to erase some of the lingering cigarette smoke.

Dory sat across from them, shaking her head. "I am still trying to process it. I mean, the fire and then her…" She swallowed. "Murder. I keep thinking it will make sense if I say it enough. She was murdered, wasn't she?"

"Yes," Ella said.

"Reed's behind it?"

"Most likely."

She gazed out the window into the darkening sky. "My sister was always so hardheaded, selfish. I tried to tell her Reed was after her money but she wouldn't listen. It seemed like he sucked all her common sense away. He led her like a sheep to the slaughter and no one on this earth could knock any sense into her."

Ella took a breath. "She wanted me to tell you… she wanted you to know that she told the truth."

"How's that?"

"I'm not sure. Maybe in her conversation with Owen and me."

"Before she tried to incinerate you?" Dory's tone was acid.

Ella tried again. "I'm not sure exactly what she meant, but I needed to tell you that she wanted forgiveness. She craved it in those last moments before her death." Ella fought a sting of tears. Owen's arm tightened around her.

Dory paced the small room. "She was terrible to me and all I wanted to do was help her."

"I think she appreciated how you tried, deep down."

"How can you tell?"

Ella chose her words carefully. "Because you were the only person on her mind just before she died."

Dory's face crumpled and she sobbed into a tissue. Ella got up to hug her and Owen retreated into the other part of the office. She didn't know if it was to allow them privacy or from discomfort at the display of emotion. When Dory had gotten control again, she thanked Ella and wiped her eyes.

"Will the police ever be able to pin anything on Bruce Reed?"

"I don't know," Ella said.

"I remembered that a young man came up, maybe a month or two ago. He was good-looking, handsome, dressed in nice clothes for these parts. He wanted to talk to my sister, but she refused."

"What was his name?"

Her brow crinkled in concentration. "Duke... no, Luke. I didn't catch the last name."

Ella exchanged a stricken look with Owen. Luke Baker had been here investigating Linda Ferron? Was it why Reed had murdered him?

"We're not going to rest until Reed gets what's coming to him," Owen interjected.

Dory sucked in a breath. "Wait a minute. I have something for you." She rummaged through the file drawer and pulled out a legal-sized envelope. Ella took it, startled to see her own address on the front with the trailer park as the return address.

"There wasn't enough postage, only one crumpled stamp, so it came back to me."

The envelope itself had been used before, the old address crossed out with a hurried hand. The handwriting was scrawled in pencil, almost illegible. Ella unsealed the flap and scanned the contents. Blood pounded in her ears and her skin prickled all over.

"What is it?" Owen asked, grabbing her wrist.

"It's a letter from Linda, written on a scrap of paper. She must have dropped it in the mailbox before she was hit by the car." Ella pulled something else out of the envelope—a key tied on a ratty red string.

"For a safe deposit box?" Owen asked.

Dory squinted. "No, mailbox, I think. One of those kinds you rent from a packaging place. I didn't know she had one. What does the letter say?"

"It's hard to read some of it, but I think…" She fought to breath. "I think Linda wrote all the things she suspects about Bruce Reed."

Dory blinked. "She really did tell the truth."

"Is it enough to have Reed arrested?" Owen said.

"Not sure, but I have a feeling whatever is in this post office box might be." She squinted at the key. "It says Parcel and Postage. I think that's a chain of stores. We can look up the address of the closest one."

Owen snapped his head toward the window, hastening over and pulling back the curtain.

Ella's nerves tightened. "What is it?"

"I don't see anyone, but I'm sure I heard a noise." He let the curtain fall into place. "Let's get back to the ranch and call Larraby before we do any more sleuthing."

As Ella drove, Owen read as much as he could from the letter. The writing was messy and hurried, and some spots were blurred and the paper warped as if she had been crying. "She's listed Lancelot and the date she purchased him, his previous owner, etc. How much she got in the insurance settlement when he died from 'colic.' She has that in quotes." Bile rose in his throat. "Maybe Bruce arranged for someone to kill Trailblazer in a way that mimics death from colic." He stared. "Does that ring any bells for you?"

Ella's skin paled to an even lighter shade. "You don't suppose he arranged the same scenario for other horses too? Like Trailblazer?"

"It got Macy out of her financial trouble at the perfect moment." He scanned the pages. "No people listed but there are five other names here, Double T, Winston, Firecracker, Hot Cocoa, Nibbles. They sound like horses. Maybe others who Reed arranged to have killed for a cut of the insurance money?" He sat forward as he read the next blurred phrase. "It says, 'see taped conversations' and there's a string of dates." Electric sparks coursed through his muscles. "That's it. That must be what's in the post office box. She recorded conversations they had where he admitted to arranging for the horses to be killed."

"Would that be admissible in court?"

"Maybe not, but it's enough to launch a formal investigation that will bring in the insurance people. Toughest marine drill sergeant I ever had was a former insurance investigator."

She squeezed the wheel. "It's almost too much to believe that we might actually have proof. It might not help my case, but at least people will be looking into Bruce Reed's activities."

"It's about time something went our way."

Rain spattered the windshield and clouds darkened the sky prematurely. The storm arrived in earnest as they turned onto the gravel drive to Gold Bar Ranch.

"See? What did I tell you about the weather? You…" he began as a gunshot split the air. He was out of the truck and running before the echo died away. The gunshot had come from the house.

"Mama," Owen shouted as he pounded across the porch and kicked open the door. He almost fell over Keegan, sprawled facedown on the area rug.

Legs quaking, he dropped to his knees, Ella scrambling to his side.

"He's breathing," Owen whispered.

"I'll stay with him. Go."

He crept into the kitchen where he found no signs of struggle. "Mama?" he called softly.

"Back here," came her strained voice. Relief and fear stampeded inside his gut as he sprinted down the hall to the master bedroom. He found his mother holding his rifle, cheeks tearstained, the back bedroom door open to the small outside porch, curtain billowing in.

He ran to her and she gripped his hand, and he took the rifle from her shaking fingers.

"I'm okay. Someone, a young man with dark hair…"

"Tony," he said through gritted teeth.

"He took Betsy." She gulped back a sob. "He came in and hauled her right out of the chair and tossed her over his shoulder. I got off one shot at his vehicle, but I was afraid I might hit her. What are we going to do?"

He took her in his arms. "Did you call the police?"

She nodded, sniffling against his chest. "Poor Betsy," she cried. "Poor thing. If I'd just acted faster."

He did his best to comfort her, but his mind was on Keegan.

"Mama, stay here, okay?"

"Why?" she demanded, eyes narrow. "What is it?"

He knew it would do no good to lie. "Keegan's hurt."

She pulled out of his arms and ran to the kitchen as he hustled after her.

Keegan was sitting up, groaning, with Ella's hand on his arm. Owen let loose with a breath. "You okay, Keeg?"

"No," he said with venom. "Coward hit me from behind."

Ella turned a stricken look at him. "Tell me," she breathed.

How he desperately wished he did not have to say it but he could not lie to her. Not now, not ever. "Ella, Tony has Betsy."

She started to shake and he went to her while his mother knelt beside Keegan. He helped her into a chair where she sat shivering, lips moving, but no sound coming out. Grabbing a blanket, he draped it around her shoulders.

He texted Jack, made sure the police were on their way, stayed close to Ella, and berated himself for not anticipating Tony's brazen move. It must have been him following them to Dory's place. He'd seen them leave with an envelope, maybe even listened in under the open trailer window and heard about Linda's notes and the key. One phone call to Reed and they'd decided on a plan.

Ella's phone rang, but she did not seem to notice so he answered it.

"If you tell the cops about what Linda gave you, Betsy dies."

TWENTY-THREE

"Reed," Owen said, fire erupting in his chest. "You tell your man Tony if Betsy so much as breaks a fingernail…"

Ella was frantically gesturing, so he turned on the speakerphone. "I want my sister. Don't hurt her. I'll do anything."

"You'll bring me Linda's papers and you don't make copies for the police. And the key. I want it all. I'll call you soon and tell you when and where. I have people watching, so don't think you can double-cross me. Do exactly what I say, or she dies, slowly and painfully." His tone went soft and smooth. "You believe that I'll do it, don't you, Ella? Luke underestimated me and that was his last mistake."

"Yes," she whispered. "I believe you. Don't hurt her. Please."

"The cops will be at your house soon, I would imagine. They'll go after Tony, but I have an alibi and they won't be able to make a connection to me. If they get wind of this phone call or one look at that envelope, you know what will happen."

Owen felt as if he was going to crush the phone. "Reed, you're going down."

"It's so hard to be the hero when you don't have a leg to stand on, isn't it?" Laughing, Reed disconnected.

Ella took the phone, staring as if it was a snake. "He's going to kill her if I don't do what he says."

"You can't trust him, Ella. He's just trying to scare you off. We have to tell the police."

She shook her head. "He means it."

"The police have the resources and manpower to handle this, Ella. We have to tell them."

"No," she shouted so loudly that Keegan and Evie both stared at her. "I have to save my sister. I have to save her. You can't tell the cops." She stared wildly from Evie to Keegan to Owen. "Please."

"It's not the right choice," he said.

"But it's my choice, Owen." Her eyes burned. "It's my sister whose life is on the line and I have to give her the best chance to survive." She got up and pressed her forehead against his chest. He closed his eyes, the sensation almost overwhelming his senses.

"Please," she whispered.

You can't negotiate with terrorists, he wanted to tell her. *Reed has no reason to keep your sister alive after he gets what he wants.* She could already be dead for all they knew. But the soft touch, the pleading in her tone, and his heart was doing flip-flops.

He wrenched his gaze from her to his mother and brother.

Slowly Evie nodded. "We will abide by her decision."

Keegan sighed. "I don't trust the cops to dispense the proper punishment anyway. We'll figure out where Reed has Betsy."

Owen turned back to Ella. "Once we go down this path, there's no turning back. Are you sure, Ella Jo? Very sure?"

"No," she said, tears rolling down her face. "I'm not sure of anything, but I have to do what he says." She swallowed convulsively. "Betsy must be terrified. I can't stand it."

He took her in his arms and held her tight until her tears soaked the front of his T-shirt and her sobs echoed in his ears.

Mr. Thorn and Jack returned from their errand to town, beating the cops by only a few minutes. Evie was tending to Keegan, who held an ice pack to his head. Ella's lungs would not cooperate, and she was sure Larraby would know she was hiding something. It was painful to know that Evie and Keegan were withholding evidence to keep Betsy alive, but not as excruciating as the knowledge that her darling sister, Betsy, was out there somewhere, scared, bewildered, in the hands of a killer.

Keegan was explaining to the police how the abduction had taken place. "I saw an SUV parked near the paddock," Keegan said. "Didn't look familiar so I came in from the stables to check and someone bashed me over the head."

Evie handed him a fresh ice pack since he had vociferously refused a trip to the emergency room. "Not your fault. I was on my way down the hall with a blanket for Betsy when this Tony knocked me down and barreled into the bedroom. He locked the door. I ran to get the key and call the police. By the time I got the door open, he had her over his shoulder and carried her out the door."

Larraby and his team took prints and photographs. "We'll get this information out as quickly as possible." His expression was soft, almost sympathetic. "I know you're worried, but we'll do everything we can to get her back, okay?"

Ella could only nod.

"Call me if you think of anything else."

Anything else? Like a madman has my sister? She was surprised he could not hear the frantic pounding of her pulse, or see the fingernails dug into the skin of her palms.

Larraby finally left. Evie and Tom sat down to puzzle over Linda's letter and the decision was made to use their small machine to make copies in spite of Reed's ultimatum. Backup insurance,

Ella thought with a pang of terror, in case he got what he wanted and didn't return her sister.

Ella did not know what to do after that, but Owen and Jack each began making calls after a quick discussion.

"What are you doing?"

"Just checking to see if anyone caught sight of Tony's vehicle leaving our property. Ken Arroyo might have gotten a look, or maybe Oscar." Both men had properties that backed the ranch. He caressed her shoulders. "Don't worry. We're not giving out any particulars and both of them can be trusted. If Tony didn't take the main highway, then the backroads would lead him either up into the mountains or north to Misery Flats."

Her stomach squeezed into a tight ball. Misery Flats was a former boomtown, abandoned after the gold went dry. Now it was acres of sun-baked ruins, a sprawl of danger and decay. She gritted her teeth and waited, each second passing in slow motion.

"I've flown over it many times. Only one main road in and out. Good hiding place," Jack said.

After a series of phone calls, the men had nothing to report. With the rain and ranch chores to be tended, no one had seen Tony's vehicle.

She checked her cell phone every few seconds to see if Reed had called but the screen remained empty. How long would he wait, letting her writhe in worry about her sister?

The evil gleam on his face when he'd nearly strangled her resurfaced.

She dies slowly and painfully. He would not have the slightest qualm about killing Betsy.

Evie tried to get everyone to sit and eat from a plate of sandwiches, but no one, not even Keegan, took her up on the offer. Ella tried desperately to keep her mind from running into terrified splinters, but she could not focus on anything except the phone in her hand, the precious envelope she refused to put down and the key she'd hung around her neck. Reed *had* to call.

Owen touched the top of her head and bent to whisper in her ear. "It's gonna be okay."

The floodgates opened and tears coursed down her face. She stood and he embraced her, smoothing her hair, talking softly to her.

A blast of cold air circled the room as someone opened the front door, but she almost didn't have the energy to care to look to see who it was until a familiar voice boomed through the kitchen.

"What, you all are sitting down to dinner and you didn't invite me?"

After a moment of utter shock, she ran to Ray and threw her arms around him.

When Ray finally disentangled himself from his sister, he accepted handshakes and hugs from the group. Owen clasped him in a fierce embrace.

"Did I interrupt something between you and my sister?" Ray said, stepping back.

He didn't miss the implication. "It's not like that."

"Looked a lot like that," he said, eyes narrowed.

"We had a situation."

Ray looked around at the family, confusion on his wide face. "Why does it seem like you all are gathering for a funeral around here?" His eyes narrowed. "Where's Betsy? I brought her a puzzle all the way from Iraq."

Ella swallowed and tried to force the words out. Ray watched for a moment until he grew impatient and looked to Owen. "Where is she?"

He knew Ray would not want any sugarcoating. "She was kidnapped about two hours ago."

Outwardly he did not react, but Owen knew his best friend enough to detect the impact of the statement had punctured him to the core. He reacted as Owen figured he would.

"What happened?" he demanded of Owen. "You were supposed to be taking care of her."

"I didn't see it coming," Owen said.

"It was your duty to see it coming," he snapped.

"I don't think you could have done better."

Ray's nostrils flared. "Oh, I think you're wrong about that. It was on your watch."

"No," Ella said. "It was on my watch."

He and Ray stared at her.

"If you'd both get off your manly high horses

and listen for a minute. Betsy is my responsibility and we are not some mission for you show-offs to argue over. Bruce Reed had his guy, Tony, abduct Betsy. We have to save her, that is, if you're both done pointing fingers at each other."

Ray finally nodded. "My rifle's at the house. I'll get her back. Where's he got her?"

"We don't know yet," Owen said.

"Cops?"

Owen explained Ella's decision not to involve them.

"Reed lives with Candy Silverton?" Ray headed for the door.

"You can't go over there," Ella said. "If you do, we'll never get Betsy back."

"Oh, I'm going to get her back, Ells." Ray's face was dark with rage.

"Listen to me," Ella pleaded to Ray's departing back.

Owen started after him.

"Nah, you stay here." Ray tossed over his shoulder. "I will take care of this myself."

Owen gripped his biceps. "You don't know what you're talking about. You don't know the players. You're gonna make things worse."

Fury darkened Ray's face. "Worse than having my sister kidnapped and Ella's life in danger? I trusted you were handling things. If I hadn't gotten leave, who knows what might have happened."

Owen clamped his jaws together. There was no defense. He had not kept the two women safe.

Ray's skin was tanned from the desert sun where he'd been sweating and risking his life daily. Owen should have been there too, his gut told him. He'd been no help to his unit, no help to Ella and Betsy. What should he say to that?

The silence stretched between them until Ray huffed out a breath. "I shouldn't be shooting my mouth off. Just venting frustration. Sorry, man. I know it's not your job to watch over my sisters 24/7."

Owen didn't answer. Not his job, but he still felt lower than he ever had.

"Got your message that you're re-upping," Ray said. His eyes swiveled to Ella. "Is that still the plan or have your priorities changed?"

His friend's innuendo ignited a hot flush that crept up Owen's neck. Their kiss in the hospital tickled his senses again and though he wouldn't admit it, he craved more of them.

Out of the corner of his eye, he saw his mother start to say something, but Jack's touch on her shoulder stopped her. Bad enough to be embarrassed by your best friend. Far worse to have your mother step in and try to smooth things over for you.

"Ray, nothing has changed. I'm glad you can admit that this isn't Owen's fault," Ella said.

"It shouldn't have been on him." Ray turned towards his sister. "I wasn't here when you needed me, but I'm here now, and I'm gonna make this Reed guy tell me where my sister is."

Ella clutched at his arm. "Ray, you can't sweep into town and take charge of everything."

"Oh, that's exactly what I'm gonna do." Ray headed for the door.

Owen knew there would be no stopping Ray short of physically taking him down. If that's what he needed to do to keep his friend from signing Betsy's death warrant, he'd do it.

"No," Owen said, beating him to the front door, "you're not."

Ray sized him up. "So that's the way it's gonna be? You're gonna take me on rather than face Reed? I never figured you for a coward, Owen. What changed?"

"I got smarter. Learned something about self-control."

"You learned how to give up."

"This isn't Afghanistan and you can't solve this problem with a half-baked rescue mission."

"Yeah? Well, you sure haven't solved anything with all this amazing self-control, have you? Ella's still going to endure a trial for murder and Betsy's gone."

"We have intel now from one of the women Reed destroyed, at least enough to make him desperate. He'll do anything to get his hands on it, and that gives us a bargaining chip."

"I'll take a fist over a chip any day." He stepped back and raised his arms in a fighting stance. "Let's get this done, Owen, so I can take care of business."

Ella cried out. "No, this is crazy. Stop it, both of you."

The shine of approaching headlights brought the conversation to a dead stop.

Owen shaded his eyes from the glare. *What now?* he thought. What else could possibly happen? He prayed the new arrival would bring some good news. He didn't see how it could possibly get any worse.

TWENTY-FOUR

Ella was dumbfounded to see Candy Silverton climb out of her car, pulling a hood over her head as she ran for the porch.

She looked up at Ella's brother. "Is that you, Ray?" Candy squinted at him. "I didn't know you were back in the States."

"Yes, ma'am," he said. "I'm on leave for a couple of weeks."

Owen ushered her in. "We've, uh, had some trouble."

"I know. I listen to the police scanner." She looked at Ella who expected to see rage or maybe even celebration in her eyes. Instead she saw an emotion she could not identify.

"Who abducted Betsy?" Candy said.

"Tony," Ella said, her tone as strong as she could make it. "But he acted on orders from Reed."

There was no denial or excuses from Candy Silverton this time, and Ella wondered what had changed.

Candy's eyes shifted in thought as Evie gestured her into a chair and poured her a cup of hot coffee.

Candy accepted the coffee with a weary smile. "Why? Why would he take Betsy?"

Owen looked at Ella. She had a split second to decide whether or not to trust Candy. Something in her manner made Ella think the alliances had shifted and Candy might possibly have had a change of heart about her beau. Owen's tiny nod confirmed her impression.

Ella sucked in a deep breath. It occurred to her that if Reed really did have people watching the house, he would know that Candy was talking to them, but there was nothing she could do about that. "I have a written statement that implicates Reed in insurance fraud, specifically the killing of horses for profit." She hesitated for one more moment. "And we also know that your nephew Luke visited Linda Ferron before her death, fruitlessly looking for information about Reed."

Candy clasped the mug tightly. "I came to tell you that I found some of Luke's papers, scraps really. He was a messy fellow." A sad smile curved her lips. "I learned he had contacted a private eye. Maybe he decided on that after he got nowhere with Linda. I phoned the detective. Luke paid him a deposit but never contacted him again." Her mouth twisted. "Because he'd already been murdered, by Tony or…" She closed her eyes. "I'm beginning to think perhaps by Bruce himself."

Ella fought for control. "I'm sorry, Mrs. Silverton. I know you loved him, but he's not the man he's pretending to be, and now he has my sister."

"I am not sure what to do," Candy said. "It's an unfamiliar feeling for me. I am usually quite certain of my decisions, but now…"

"We're waiting for him to contact us," Owen put in. "Do you know where he is?"

Her reply seemed to take a very long time. "He came home a few hours ago, just before I found the private eye's number. I asked him about his late wife and why he hadn't told me about her. He said it was too painful, the train wreck and losing her." She drummed on the coffee cup. "So sincere. You'd never guess it was anything but the purest truth."

"So he's at your home? Now? Is it possible he'll have Betsy brought there?" She was grasping at straws and she knew it. He was not stupid enough to have a disabled woman carried onto his girlfriend's property and risk someone noticing.

Candy's eyes shifted in thought. "After our talk, he said he had to attend to a business matter with the broodmares. I demanded to see them and he said he'd arrange it, but I'm beginning to think he's not going to let me see those horses. They're probably worth nothing."

"But Doc Potter checked them over."

She lifted a shoulder. "Bruce probably showed him the wrong horses. I have a feeling the ones I put a deposit on aren't worth nearly what I paid, but I'm putting pressure on Bruce now so he has to come up with something. I told him if I don't see them with my own eyes in the next twenty-four hours, I'm calling off the sale. He agreed to my deadline. Said he'd be back tomorrow."

Reed was gone for twenty-four hours? Was he planning on returning after he'd gotten his hands on the evidence? *And killed her sister?* She swallowed. At least she could rest easy that Ray could not force a confrontation and get himself killed.

The desperation of their situation crashed in on her full-on. Reed had no way of ensuring that they wouldn't act against his wishes and distribute copies of Linda's claims to the police. The only leverage he had was Betsy's life. Maybe Owen had been right—they should have told the police everything. Cold seeped deep into her bones. She realized Candy was looking at her.

"I'm sorry," Candy said. "I didn't want to think Bruce was responsible. It was…less painful to blame it on you."

Ella took her hand, clutching at the scant comfort of having Candy believe her. "He fooled all of us."

Candy tightened her grip. "What should I do? How can I help you find Betsy?"

"Gather anything in your home that we could

use as evidence against him," Ella said. "Maybe Luke made other notes. We'll present it to the police if…when…"

"*When* we get Betsy back," Owen finished. "In the meantime, don't let Reed back into your house. If he returns, text me right away and don't contact the police." He gave her his cell number.

Candy pulled her jacket around her. "There's one more thing you should know." Her expression was grim.

Ella braced herself for the next blow.

"Bruce left with a pair of hiking boots and jeans, as if he was planning on being outside."

Outside? Possibly on his way to Misery Flats?

"And…and he took something else with him."

"What?"

"A gun."

Owen listened carefully as they laid out their plans by the flickering firelight. Rain pounded on the roof of the Gold Bar, and the scent of wood smoke and coffee drifted in the air. Owen felt a sense of relief that they were finally going to take the offensive, get to Misery Flats and conduct their own search to find Betsy before Reed set up the exchange.

"Rain's supposed to stop in the next couple of hours," Owen said.

Ray nodded. "We'll go before then. Sunrise is at oh six hundred, and we'll be in place before that. Flashlights, rifles, radios." He shot a look at Ella. "We can move out the back and Reed won't see us, even if he has people watching, which I think was a bluff anyway. You and Mrs. Thorn stay here in case there's any info from the cops."

"No." Ella folded her arms across her chest. "I'm coming."

"Uh-uh," Ray said.

Owen could have told Ray that he had zero chance of ordering his sister to stay back, but Ray forged ahead anyway until Ella cut him off, with fire in her eyes.

"Do you know how to soothe Betsy, Ray? Do you know how to help her drink water when the muscles of her throat tighten up? When was the last time you massaged the kinks out of her calves or calmed her when she has a nightmare about things she can't communicate?"

His mouth opened then shut and he had the decency to look chagrined. "Okay. I get it. I'm sorry, sis. You're with me. Jack and Keegan together."

"On horseback," Jack said. "There's a horse trail in from the back Reed probably doesn't know about."

Ray gave him a startled look, then a nod. "Good. Tony won't even hear you coming. Tom and Evie can stay here and call for backup if we need it."

Owen felt the insult as Ray intended. "And me?"

"You watch the road in and out. Alert if there's any traffic."

He wanted to argue, to insist that he be there at Ella's side, but Ray didn't want him anywhere close to his sister. Owen knew he was justified at some level. Owen was distracted by her presence, by her spirit, by that soul that danced inside her and made him want to be different, better. The reality of it reared up inside him. Somewhere along the trail, his friendship with the freckle-faced Ella had morphed into love.

Had that love distracted him from keeping her safe? Had his burning desire to return to the marines preoccupied him from devoting himself fully to her protection? It didn't matter why, he told himself savagely. He hadn't helped convict Bruce Reed and he hadn't prevented Tony from taking Betsy. What had he done exactly, but secure his return to duty and witnessed Ella's descent into a state of desperation that threatened to drown her?

"Affirmative," he said quietly, avoiding Ella's gaze.

They lingered by the fireside, putting together supplies. Owen made sure his rifle was clean and fully loaded. There would be no shots fired unless absolutely necessary, they had all agreed. He knew his brothers would be extra cautious, but he could not be quite as certain about Ray. He was hungry for revenge at the wrongs visited on his family.

As he filled up some water bottles at the kitchen tap, he felt Ella next to him.

"Ray's just upset and he defaults to this kind of behavior when he can't manage his emotions."

Owen smiled. "Been there, done that. I get it. He's right anyway. I should have anticipated Reed's level of desperation."

"No one can anticipate a crazy person's actions."

Her small face shone up at him with such faith, such trust, that his breath caught. He capped the water bottles and allowed himself to trace a finger over the perfect curve of her cheek.

"I'm sorry, Ella. I let you down, just like Ray said."

"No, you didn't. None of this is your fault."

All of it is, he thought. *I love you and I'm leaving you.* At that moment he wanted to kiss her again, like he had in the hospital room, to find that perfect connection that restored him like no medicine or victory ever had. He ached at the distance between them, only inches that would soon be meters, continents, years.

Ray came up, taking one of the water bottles. "Ella, it's time to go. Evie wants to talk to you first."

She nodded and left the kitchen.

Ray's jaw was set into a hard line. "We'll straighten this out and she can have her life back."

He didn't speak.

"She deserves that, a normal life, with a guy who will be there for her."

Not like you, Owen.

Ray gave an apologetic shrug. "It's nothing personal, man, but she's my sister and like we always said, guys like us are built for war, not for weddings."

Owen heard Ella's voice in his memory.

You're made for more than that.

But his dream, his desire to return to the marines would take first place in his heart, like it always had.

Picking up his rifle, he moved out into the storm-soaked night.

TWENTY-FIVE

Ella clung to the armrest as Ray's truck bounced up the steep trail toward Misery Flats, jarring her spine and rattling her teeth. A heavy fringe of pines blackened the path even more. It was almost one o'clock in the morning, and she fought against the fatigue that came in alternating waves with the terror. When they got to the top, he turned off the headlights. Her brother had excellent night vision, but she still held her breath until they rolled to a stop behind an enormous pile of granite boulders. Ray turned on the radio, speaking softly.

"Marine?"

"All clear here," Owen answered.

"Brothers?"

Jack's quiet voice chimed in. "Approaching the south trail. We'll be another twenty minutes. Footing's slippery."

"Copy that." Ray clicked off the radio. "I'm going to check things out."

She held up a hand. "Don't even bother to tell

me to stay put." She zipped her jacket and pulled the black ski cap over her red hair. "Let's go."

"And I thought I was the tough one."

"You thought wrong."

They climbed out, closing the car doors carefully. Scrambling onto the pile of rocks, they got a view of the town of Misery Flats spread out before them. Ella remembered from a long-ago school report that Misery Flats had once been home to more than 2,000 buildings and a population of close to 7,000 people before other booms in Montana, Arizona and Utah lured wealth seekers away.

Now many of the buildings were collapsed, swallowed up by decay and debris, but hundreds were still upright, some hugging the dirt road which had turned to mud that wound along the hillside. The facade of the brick buildings had fared better than the wooden structures, standing tall in the rain. The acres spread out before them, and Ella felt her spirit fall. It had been hours since her sister had been taken. Hours with no food, water, without even her wheelchair. Ella swallowed hard and mouthed a prayer.

"Where do we start?"

"There." Ray pointed to a boxy two-story brick structure. "Old schoolhouse. We can get an excellent view from the roof."

The walls gleamed wetly in the rain. Ella wondered how sturdy the structure was after centuries of blazing Gold Country sun and the damp winter conditions.

Ray hitched the rifle by a strap over his shoulder and grabbed hold of the iron ladder, which led past the second level to the roof that would indeed provide the perfect lookout. The metal groaned under his weight, so they decided she should not add to the load by climbing up after.

The wind moaned around them, spattering her with water droplets that snaked down the back of her jacket, sending her shivering. Was Betsy cold? Was she at least out of the driving rain? Were they even looking in the right spot? Again she checked her phone, which still showed no calls from Reed or anyone else. Only a text from Owen.

I'm here.

How comforting were those two words. With her brother and Owen at her side, she felt a slight twinge of hope that maybe, just maybe, they could find Betsy before Ella was forced to hand over the envelope and key.

Ray was halfway up the ladder, climbing easily. One second he was ascending, and then there was a shriek of metal, followed by a horrible ear-splitting groan as the ladder separated from the crumbling brick and came crashing to the earth.

She screamed and ran to her brother. At first she could not find him until she heard a groan a few yards away. She ran to the edge of a ravine. Ray lay at the bottom, leg splayed at an awkward angle.

Clutching the radio she frantically messaged. "Ray's fallen." Not waiting for a reply, she scrambled down to him, heedless of the rocks and twisted roots that caught at her.

"Ray," she panted. He was on his side, face contorted with pain, his rifle fallen a few feet away. "How bad is it?"

He grimaced and rolled onto his back. "I'm all right."

She didn't believe it for a moment. Running her hands along his arms and neck, she checked for anything out of alignment or the warm feel of blood. She found nothing until she started in on his legs. When she touched his right ankle, he clamped his lips together to keep from crying out.

"Broken?" she breathed.

"Nah, just a sprain. Give me a minute. I'll be okay."

After some labored breathing, he sat up and shook the dirt from his hair. "See? I told you I'm fine."

She decided not to disagree with him. A quiet scrunch of boots against the ground sent her heartbeat skittering.

"My gun," Ray breathed. "Can you get it?"

She was halfway there when a voice called out.

"It's me, Ella." Owen crouched next to Ray. "Fine time for a rest break."

"I don't need your help." He shot a glance at Ella. "You shouldn't have called him."

"Can't unspill the milk, as my father says," Owen said, keeping his voice quiet. "Can you walk on it?"

"Of course I can walk on it." Ray did accept Owen's hand with obvious reluctance. As soon as he put weight on the ankle, it gave out and he would have gone down again if Owen hadn't held him up.

"Mission's over for you, Ray. I'll take you back to the truck." His voice held the tiniest note of mischief. "You can take over my job as lookout."

Ray fumed. "I'm not leaving Ella."

"Then she can sit in the truck with you."

Now Ella gave him a look similar to her brother's. "I…" Her phone buzzed. Every ounce of warmth drained from her as she saw Reed's message glowing on the screen.

Owen felt Ray's grip on his shoulder tighten like a vise. The weight of his big friend sent a pulse of pain through his still-injured shoulder, which he ignored.

"Ella?"

"It's Reed. He said to meet him at the old stamp mill with the key and Linda's notes or he'll kill Betsy."

Owen experienced the surreal calm he always felt when he knew he was about to walk into the chaos of battle. "Give them to me. I'll go and meet him."

"No, he will be looking for me."

Owen and Ray both started to argue at the same time, but she simply shook her head. "The mill is just around the bend in the road. I'm going."

Owen led a struggling Ray back to his truck and half shoved him in the front seat. Ray gripped his forearm. "Don't let her down."

Don't let her die, is what he really meant.

He left his stricken friend behind the wheel with his rifle and the radio. "Call the cops if I say so. Get them here quick." That would mean Ella's brash plan to get her sister back had failed. He knew from grim experience it might have failed already, and Betsy may have already been murdered.

He closed the truck door, radioed his brothers, and caught up with Ella, who was marching through the wet scrub to avoid the road where she would be easily seen. The key gleamed on the string around her neck.

He took her hand and she turned to look at him. "I didn't want your help."

"I know."

"But I'm grateful to have it."

He squeezed her cold fingers in reply. The magnificent strength of Ella Cahill took his breath away. She was scared, terrified, yet she would face down any danger or difficulty for her sister. The responsibility she'd thought to escape as a teenager had turned out to be the very thing that had transformed her into what God wanted her to be. Betsy was no burden; she was a path of life that God had chosen for Ella, instead of the one she'd chosen for herself.

They slowed on the last swell of hill, hunkering down between a rickety chapel, panes of glass beside the door still partially intact, and an enormous pile of what must have been a general store. Now it was nothing more than a ten-foot-high pile of wood and brick with some graffiti scrawled across it by some modern-day trouble seekers.

Owen used his binoculars to scan the stamp mill. It was a tall four-story structure made of wood that had decayed in some spots, leaving access for wildlife and the elements. No signs of life.

The mill had been used during Misery Flats' heydays to crush the gold ore into a powder, which was treated with mercury to remove the gold. Up close the stamp mill was no more than a rusted shell, filled with the relics of a bustling industry. Some sort of night flier, perhaps a bat or an owl, swept past them into one of the gaping holes in the siding. The smell of wet iron and rust permeated the damp air.

"I'll go by myself from here," she said.

"No way."

"If I…if we don't come out, you can get him."

"Ella Jo," he said, rifle ready in his hands. "You're gonna give me five minutes, and I'm gonna make entry into that stamp mill without him even knowing it." His plan was that Ella would not have to walk through those moldering doors at all. "You down with the plan?"

She quirked an exasperated smile. "Does it matter?"

"Nope." He leaned over before he could second-guess himself and pulled her to him, his mouth fitting perfectly to hers as if she was made for him, a match, body and soul. He sought a kiss for courage, for comfort, yet the feelings that bubbled up inside were so much deeper that it made his head spin until they broke the kiss.

He pulled her hood over her hair. "Gonna rain," he said hoarsely. "Doppler says eighty percent."

She did not reply, but he could tell she was breathing hard, perhaps as off-kilter as he was.

"Five minutes," he said. Not able to stand another moment of those wondering eyes, he put his head down and crept toward the mill.

Ella crouched in the tall weeds, wishing she could sit and allow her limbs to quiet. Owen. His kiss soldered her spirit to his with an indelible bond. She would love him until her dying day, beyond the hurt of him leaving her again, past the pain of this uncertain moment, however tragically it might turn out.

"Please," she murmured to God. "Please." It was all she could manage, but He knew her deepest yearnings, for Owen, for Betsy, for herself.

The minutes ticked by on her watch, one then three. She hadn't heard a single sound but the frigid wind, her own tense breathing and the faraway howl of a coyote.

Four minutes. Five.

On shaky legs, she stood and texted Reed.

I'm here.

His response came immediately.

Do you have what I want?

Her fingers shook. Yes. Papers and key.

"Good," he said, stepping out from behind the ruins of the general store.

She spun around, her blood freezing.

He smiled. "The look on your face. Priceless. Did you think I was going to let your cowboy truss me up like a turkey while you stood outside and watched the fun?"

"I did what you said. I want my sister."

He scanned the area, dark eyes unreadable. "I feel a little exposed out here, considering how many brothers your cowboy has. I've never been one for the wide-open spaces anyway. We'll go inside."

Fear ratcheted up a level. Why would he risk confronting Owen unless...

Reed laughed. "Oh, I think Tony will have probably finished up with him by now, but just in case..." He pulled a gun from his pocket and hefted it in his hand. "Funny isn't it, how even the smallest of guns can make such a deadly hole?"

The whites of his eyes glinted.

Owen! her mind screamed, but she would not give him the satisfaction of seeing her desperation. "Where's my sister?"

He gestured with the gun for her to precede him into the mill. "Why don't we go find out?"

TWENTY-SIX

Owen's nose twitched at the smell of mildew that permeated the old mill. Crouching behind a haphazard pile of wood, he allowed his eyes to adjust, and then he went completely still, listening. As a new marine, he'd been too eager, bold to the point of brashness. If God had taught him anything through his deployments and the situation with Ella, it was the power of patience. Excruciatingly hard as it was, he stayed immobile, honing in on the smallest sound.

The crouched position aggravated his leg, but he remained, until at long last he was rewarded by the quiet creak of a floorboard. He looked around the aged stamp machine that was rusted in place and saw Tony, peering at his phone. Owen aimed the rifle.

"Game over, Tony," he said, emerging from cover.

But Tony seemed not at all surprised by his appearance and ducked immediately behind an

enormous bin, pulling a gun from his waistband
and firing off a round that pinged into the metal
near Owen's head. From somewhere he heard a
scream. Ella? He dove for cover and loosed a few
rounds of his own. The rifle bullets punched into
and through the metal walls of the bin and drove
Tony out the other side as Owen had hoped. This
time Owen aimed close enough that the bullet
whistled past Tony's left ear, sending him to the
ground, hands covering his head. Owen was on
him in a second, boot coming down hard on Tony's wrist until he let go of the gun.

Owen kicked it away. "Get up."

Tony did, mouth twisted into a sullen line.

"Where's Betsy?"

Tony glared. "Not gonna tell you anything."

"You're going to go to jail for running down
Linda Ferron and for Betsy's kidnapping. At least
make it easier on yourself by helping us find her."

"Not going to prison."

"You think Reed's gonna bail you out? He lets
you do the dirty work and he profits. You're nothing to him. You handed over the thermos to him,
didn't you?"

Silence. Owen shifted, once again listening. Tony's lack of surprise at his arrival set off Owen's
mental alarm. He wondered where his brothers
were. There was still no sound to indicate Reed
was in the mill somewhere. Owen figured him for

the type who would not put himself at risk when he could command his subordinate to do it.

"Did you kill Luke Baker too, Tony? Do you do everything Reed tells you?" He shook his head. "What kind of a man are you?"

A floorboard creaked and Owen tensed, rifle still trained on Tony as Ella stumbled forward into the space, propelled by a shove from Bruce Reed.

"He's the kind of man," Reed said, "who does what he's told and makes a good living at it. He's about to head off for a nice long vacation to Mexico, aren't you, Tony? As a matter of fact, we both are, as soon as I make sure there won't be a pack of insurance investigators following me and I close a horse deal I've been working on." Reed gestured with the gun at Ella's back. "Your weapon on the floor, Owen, or my trigger finger will start to get antsy." Owen could see the tension in Reed's gloved hands.

Ella stood, hugging herself, eyes wide. *I'm sorry,* she mouthed.

Not your fault, he wanted to say. They knew it might be a setup and they were right. They still had his brothers and Ray as backup.

"You're not getting out of here," Owen said. "Candy knows the truth."

He glowered. "The rifle, on the floor now." Reed pushed the gun to the back of Ella's head and she flinched. Fury sprang to life inside him, but he fought it back. *Control. Wait for the moment. Keep him from hurting her.*

"And I *am* getting out of here. Your backup, the guy in the truck? He's not close enough to help or even hear the shots."

But he hadn't mentioned Jack and Keegan. Owen played for time. "He's already called the cops."

"Then I better get a move on. Rifle. Floor. Now." He pressed his gun so hard to Ella's head that she grimaced.

Pulse raging, Owen slid his rifle to the floor and Tony snatched it up, grinning. Reed gestured for it and pocketed his own gun to take possession.

"Like candy from a baby," Reed said, cradling Owen's rifle. "Let's cut to the chase. Give me what I asked for."

"It won't matter anyway," Ella said. "We made copies of Linda's letter. We'll give it to the cops."

He shrugged. "The ramblings of a drunk. You haven't had time to make a copy of the key. That's all I care about. Gonna clear out this mailbox and whatever it is she caught on tape before I leave town. Linda hinted at me that she'd recorded me. I told her it would be the worst mistake of her whole sorry life." His face went tight as his free hand felt around her neck. Owen's fury almost drove him crazy. Reed found the string, yanked it from her neck and pocketed it. Reed shoved her away and she tumbled into Owen.

Owen grabbed at Ella and shoved her behind him.

"Why did you kill Luke Baker?" Ella said.

Reed laughed. "You know, I'd love to stay and have this chat, but time's growing short before the police join the party." With a blur of motion, he raised the rifle and fired.

Tony fell to the ground. A spot of red blossomed on his side. Ella screamed in horror. Owen pushed them farther away from Reed, but there was nowhere to go and soon they were backed against the metal bin.

"Why…?" Ella gasped.

"Neat, isn't it?" Reed laughed. "It's like a movie, see? Here's how the script goes. You two cornered Tony, who abducted your sister because you found some evidence that Tony killed Luke Baker. Tony pulled a gun on you, this gun," he said, taking the smaller gun from his pocket. "And shot you both. While bleeding to death, the brave Owen, being the stalwart marine, got off one rifle shot, which killed Tony. I don't think the police coroner will pinpoint the time of death precisely enough to figure out the truth."

Ella gasped. "You're a monster."

"No, I'm just a guy trying to make it in this world. I'm determined, that's all. It's enough to make Candy believe me, I figure. If not…" He shrugged. "Mexico's nice."

"My sister…"

He raised a shoulder. "Your sister will die, like you."

"No," Ella shouted. She lunged for him but Owen held her wrist.

Tears streamed down her face. "There's no reason to kill her. I'm the one you want. Leave her alone."

Reed aimed the smaller gun at them. "Betsy is such a delicate flower, Ella." He smiled, wolf-like, lowering his voice to a conspiratorial whisper. "How do you know she's not dead already?"

Ella cried out and Owen used the moment to shove her aside and launch himself right at Reed.

The scream died in Ella's throat as Owen knocked Reed over backward, the rifle flying out of his hand and skittering under a pile of rusted iron.

She ran for it.

Owen and Reed rolled over and over, grunting. Frantically, she scrambled for the gun, but it had wedged itself far under the pile and she couldn't reach it.

Turning back, she tried to spot Reed's weapon, realizing to her horror that it was now locked in the man's grip. He'd managed to get it out of his pocket. A shot rang out, sizzling through the air and ricocheting off a metal beam overhead.

"Ella," Owen gasped. She knew he was telling her to take cover, but this madman had taken her sister and she would not let him take Owen too. Snatching up a metal bar she raised it up and brought it down on the back of Reed's leg.

He howled in pain and Owen wrested the gun from his grip and leapt to his feet, breathing hard, gun trained on Reed.

"Get up," he spat.

Reed did, palms raised, eyes murderous.

Ella faced him. "Where's my sister?"

"The only way you'll ever know is if you let me go."

"No way." Owen looked from Reed to Ella. "If we let him go, he'll never tell you anyway."

Ella's mind raced. How could she let him go? How could she stand knowing she might never find her sister? Never know what Reed had done with her? Her legs shook, mind unable to process, soul unable to pray.

Betsy, Betsy.

The door was flung open. Keegan came in, leading Zeke Potter by the shoulder.

"What…?" She could not get the rest of the question out.

"I'm sorry," Zeke said. "I didn't want to."

Jack followed behind. "We heard the shot. Police are rolling."

There was a blur of motion. "Stop," Owen hollered.

Her attention snapped back just in time to see Reed bolt for a gaping hole in the wall. Owen raised the pistol he'd taken.

"No," she cried out. "I'll never find Betsy."

Owen hesitated, torn.

The second delay allowed Reed to disappear into the night.

"I'll go after him." Keegan raced toward the spot where Reed had made his escape.

Owen lowered the weapon, wiping a hand across his brow. "Call Ray," he told Jack. "And get the police to bring a search dog."

Jack nodded and made the call.

A dog? She did not understand at first, so jumbled were her thoughts. Then she was enveloped by a cloud of despair. Reed had the key and he knew where Betsy was. And he'd just made his escape. Owen was right, she knew with a sick feeling.

He'll never tell you anyway.

It had been almost twelve hours since her sister was abducted. How many more would it take to find her in this blighted ruin? Or maybe it was already too late. Far easier to hide a body...

Nausea clawed her insides. She felt the weight of Zeke's tortured gaze on her.

She went to him. "Why are you here?"

"I…" He looked down.

"He was Reed's backup. Phoning information to him," Jack said as he disconnected. "He blabbed the whole story when I intercepted him outside."

Ella could not process the statement. "You… you were helping Reed?"

Tears rolled down Zeke's face. "I had to. I owed a lot of money and he talked me into doing a job for him. Just one job. And then he owned me."

"What job?" Owen's tone was hard as granite.

Zeke didn't answer.

Owen let out a breath. "You killed horses for him, didn't you?"

Ella shook her head. "No, no, you could not have done something like that."

"I needed the money to pay back my gambling debt. It didn't hurt them. A simple electrocution. They died instantly."

"You did it to Trailblazer, Macy Gregory's horse?" Owen said.

He did not answer at first. "Reed said if I didn't help, he'd tell the cops."

"And you lied about Candy's broodmares. You told her they were good specimens."

"Yes," he whispered.

"Oh, Zeke." Ella's eyes burned but no more tears would come. "You helped Reed frame me for Luke's murder?"

"I didn't know he was gonna do that. I went along with killing horses, but people? Luke? I told him I wouldn't cooperate, that I knew it was him that killed Luke because he was going to tell Candy everything he'd found out about Reed. Reed said if I talked…" Zeke rubbed at his eyes. "I didn't want him to hurt you or Betsy. I begged him. I didn't know he'd cooked up a plan to frame you for the murder until he'd already drugged you, honest I didn't."

Ella strode up to him, forcing his chin up so he would have to look at her. "Where is my sister, Zeke? You have to tell me."

He looked at her through a veil of agony. "I don't know. Reed wouldn't let Tony tell me. I think he thought I would break down and tell. And I would have. I wouldn't have let him hurt Betsy."

Two shots rang out in the distance, each one punching a hole in Ella's heart. Had Reed gone to Betsy before he made his escape? Was her sister dead? A smothering wall of darkness began to press down on her and her legs began to shake as the cops arrived and began to dispatch various officers to investigate the shots. "So you don't know where my sister is?"

"I'm sorry." He began to sob. "I'm so sorry for everything."

TWENTY-SEVEN

The police had sent a request to Rock Ridge for a search-and-rescue dog.

"We'll find her," Larraby said.

If it's not too late. Ella began to pace in front of the derelict stamp mill. The medics were tending to Tony who was still breathing in spite of his grievous wound, and the police were recording statements from all of them after taking Zeke Potter into custody. Keegan had returned after Reed eluded him. There was no word yet from Ray, no indication of whom had fired the shots they'd heard.

Owen stood nearby, restless. They'd fanned out, calling Betsy's name until the police took over. Still Ella's body would not rest, not until they brought her sister home. She couldn't stop herself from walking, calling, entreating her sister to answer, but there was no response except the moaning of the wind.

She gazed up into the watery moonlight, her

heart crying out for Betsy. Owen came close, taking her in his arms. She didn't want to be there in the circle of his embrace, so weighted was her heart with her failure, grief and hopelessness.

But her legs would not hold her, and there seemed to be nothing keeping her together except for the strength of his touch.

The moon appeared from behind the clouds, glinting on the broken panes of glass of the old chapel. Her body vibrated with shock. She wrenched away from Owen.

"What is it, Ella?"

She could not answer. Instead, she sprinted to the chapel, praying that she had not been tricked by the light, by her own avalanche of grief.

He ran after her, almost colliding when she stopped short, shaking fingers touching the glass. There on the broken pane was a name, crudely written in the dust.

B-e-t-s-y. It showed backward, indicating her sister had written it from the inside.

She slammed into the chapel, hunting through the broken pews.

Owen did the same.

"But we already checked the building. There was no sign of her," he said.

"She's here. I know it. They left her alone long enough that she wrote her name." Ella searched again, looping in ever more frantic circles in the wrecked building.

Jack and Keegan joined in.

"They might have moved her to another location," Keegan said. She refused to believe it, pawing through piles of debris for any sign of her sister.

"Here." Owen was crouching on the filthy floor, behind the last pew. His fingers traced a grimy line cut into the wood. "Trapdoor."

All four of them dropped to their knees, searching for a handle. Jack finally found it. He yanked it open.

Body gone cold with fear and hope, Ella leaned over, hands reaching into the darkness.

A trembling palm met her own, so fragile, but it was enough to cement the pieces of her heart back together and breathe life back into her spirit.

"Betsy!" she cried out, her tears falling down onto the pale face peeking up at her. "I'm here. I'm here."

Owen and Keegan extracted Betsy from the hole as gently as they could while Jack summoned the paramedics.

Betsy was weak, unable to talk, but her pulse was strong, the medics told Ella.

A pickup blazed up the road, stopping next to the ambulance.

Ray hopped out, weight on one foot.

"She's alive," Ella said. "Betsy's alive."

He sagged in relief, wrapping his sister in a hug. Over the top of her head, he shot Owen a look.

"Mission accomplished," he said.

Owen looked at them together, Ray and his sister. Suddenly a piece slid into place in his mind, heart and soul. He knew that he was going to need to have a very important conversation with Ray Cahill—one that might very well change their lives forever. If it lost him his best friend, so be it. But now was not the time.

"Not fully accomplished," Owen said. "Reed got away."

Ray flashed them a cocky smile. "Nah. While you guys were having a picnic down here, I handled things."

Owen felt a swell of hope. "What things?"

"Look in the back of the truck."

Along with his brothers, he stared into the back of the pickup where they found Bruce Reed, bound at the wrists and ankles, silent and seething.

"Saw him making a break for his car. Knocked out the front tire with my first shot, then fired another just over his head when he got out, close enough that he knew I meant business. The rest was easy."

Owen could not hold back the laughter. "Oh you were doing the shooting we heard. Thanks for the assist."

"Anytime," Ray said, still holding his sister tight.

"I'm not going to jail," Reed snarled.

Owen leaned over the truck bed, so Reed locked

eyes with him. He wanted to make sure that Reed knew without a doubt that he was beaten and that he would never be free to poison anyone's life again. "That's where you're wrong," Owen said. "Very, very wrong."

Ella remained at Betsy's side in the hospital and Owen stayed with her, leaving only for a short while to shower and change. He didn't say much, just listened to Ella and comforted her when she cried as she relived the tumultuous events of the past few hours. Tears flowed freely when she spoke on what Zeke Potter had done.

Owen held her, stroking her exquisite red hair and thanking God that He had protected both Ella and Betsy from the enemy they'd known about and the one they hadn't.

The doctor checked in after another examination of Betsy.

"She's doing well. We've got her rehydrated and we're giving her antibiotics. She will be here for a while, but I think she's going to be okay. Right now she's enjoying a nice nap."

Ella thanked him profusely. Owen took her hand and guided her toward the elevator.

"Time for some fresh air."

"But…"

He handed her a jacket his mom had brought. "The Thorn brigade will be arriving any minute, and there's something I want to talk to you about."

"Are you bossing me?"

He stopped and touched her cheek. "No," he said softly. "I'm asking you."

She laughed. "Well, in that case, I guess a little fresh air couldn't hurt."

They found a spot outside—a quiet, landscaped area which held a gazebo tucked away next to a cluster of pine trees. It was cold, the air heavy with the promise of imminent rain and the forecast of hail.

She sucked in a deep breath, eyes closed, the delicate muscles of her neck working as she stretched. "It's good to be outside. I'm still in shock over it all."

"Seems like a lifetime ago that..." He trailed off.

"That you found me on the side of the road."

He sighed. "I didn't want to bring up bad memories."

The rain began to fall then, pattering against the gazebo roof. "It's okay. It will take me a while, but I will get over it."

"Yes, you will, Ella Jo. You're one tough cookie."

Her smile went a little sad, he thought. "I guess I am. What did you want to tell me?"

He took a breath and said it, making it real. "I'm not going back to the marines."

She gaped. "What? Why?"

"Because I'm letting it go to pursue something that God meant just for me." His pulse hammered.

"The ranch?"

"Not the ranch."

Her lips quirked in confusion. "What, then?"

He let out a shaky breath. "You, Ella. I want to stay here with you."

Her shock quickly morphed into denial. "No, Owen. I don't need you to give up the marines for me."

"I know you don't need it. This isn't about duty or obligation."

"What's it about, then?"

"Love. I love you."

She went still and quiet, eyes searching his face. He prayed she'd find the answer she needed there.

Slowly she shook her head. "You'll always resent me for it."

"I probably would have a while ago, but not anymore." He tried to put into words the feelings that had been circling in his soul. "You told me you gave up your dreams to take up His cross. I didn't understand how you could do that, give up on what you wanted so badly to follow His plan for your life. I understand now."

She touched a finger to his temple, tracing the curve of his cheekbone. "Owen, that is the sweetest thing I've ever heard, but it will hurt too much to give up your dream, for me."

"Yes, it will hurt, just like you have been hurting, and I will struggle like you have, but His plan for my life is better." He reached for her, laying his hands along her neck, thumbs caressing the silken skin. "What kind of fool would I be to turn my back on a future with the woman I love?"

Tears glinted in her eyes. "I can't let you do it."

"You're right. You can't. It has to be my decision, but not just mine. What you do have to say, Ella Jo? Do you love me?" The question made him feel helpless, caught on tenterhooks of doubt. What if…?

She began to pace in circles, heedless of the hail which had replaced the rain, tapping onto the roof above them. "Owen, I love you so much," she said in a voice so quiet he almost missed it. "I've loved you since I was a kid."

Elation swelled inside him until she turned away, arms folded around herself.

"But I'm afraid," she continued. "I'm afraid you'll stay here with me and spend your whole life missing the marines."

He picked up a piece of ice from the ground and held it up, the surface glinting in the porch light like a diamond. "Ella, did you know that new hailstones are too lightweight to fall to earth? They have to stay up in the storm, collecting water and getting bounced around like ping-pong balls until they have enough substance to fall down here."

Her expression was pained, but quizzical as he continued.

"The marines gave me substance, made me

man enough to survive the storm, but you…" He moved close and peeled her arm away from her body, stroking the soft skin on the inside of her wrist before he pressed a kiss there. "You made me want to come home and stay."

Her eyes were the green of spring grass. "Owen, are you sure?" she whispered. "Very, very sure? If you changed your mind it would…"

Break her heart. But he would live the rest of his life making sure he treated her like the precious woman she was, a woman he could not live without.

"I've never been more certain of anything else in my whole life." With effort he moved away. "But how do you feel about it, Ella? Your brother would say I'm not a fit partner. I'm a hard-bitten ex-marine with a busted-up leg and a fixation on the weather."

She smiled. "Yes, he would say that."

He felt a trickle of uncertainty. "And he'd probably be right."

She nodded slowly. "Yes, he would be."

"I've talked to him about it."

Her eyebrows arched. "Talked?"

"Well, bossed actually."

"Bossed Ray?"

"Yeah. I told him you and I were meant to be together and if he couldn't accept that—he could go soak his head," he said.

Now her eyes were wide as quarters. "How did that go over?"

He shook his head. "Doesn't matter. You are part of our family already, always have been. But now—" he sank down to one knee "—I want to make it official."

"I think it matters, Marine," came a growl from the gazebo steps. He looked up to find Ray, leaning on crutches, the hail bouncing off his baseball cap. Owen stood and faced him, chin up.

"You're not right for Ella," Ray said.

Ella started to answer, but Owen stopped her. "Due respect, Ray, you're wrong and your opinion doesn't matter here. If Ella loves me and she'll have me, I'll be the best husband I can possibly be."

"And if I still disagree?"

He shrugged. "I believe we already discussed the head soaking."

Ray's expression held firm for three seconds before he grinned, bursting into laughter. "Then I guess I'm just gonna have to give my blessing."

Owen smiled before he turned to Ella. "Ella Cahill, will you do me the honor of being my wife?"

The clatter of the hail tapered off, and for a moment the world was silent except for the wham of his heart against his ribs.

Two beats later she leapt into his arms, laughing and crying all at the same time. "Yes, Owen Thorn, I believe I will marry you."

Turning her to shield them from Ray's prying eyes, he went in for a kiss, his heartbeat joining in the joyful rhythm of the rain.

* * * * *

If you enjoyed Treacherous Trails,
look for the first book in the
GOLD COUNTRY COWBOYS *series:*
COWBOY CHRISTMAS GUARDIAN.

Available now from Love Inspired!

Find more great reads at
www.LoveInspired.com

Dear Reader,

Did you ever give up on a dream that you wanted with all your heart? That hurts, doesn't it? It's almost like experiencing a death, in a way. In *Treacherous Trails*, both Ella and Owen come to realize that God's plans for their lives are so much better than those they fashion for themselves, but the lesson is not learned without struggle and pain. That happy ending could not come a moment too soon for those two!

In this book we've gotten a closer look at Owen Thorn, the second of the Thorn brothers. It was a joy to write about a close-knit family of brothers who support each other through thick and thin. As one of four sisters, I value so much the unconditional love of my family. I hope that you have experienced that kind of unconditional love, whether via a sibling or a close friend. These are the people that hold us up when our dreams lie broken at our feet, the earthly hands and feet God uses to carry us through the darkest time until the sun shines again.

I enjoy hearing from my readers, so feel free to pop by my website at danamentink.com and leave a comment. There's a physical address there as well if you prefer to correspond via letter. Friends, I sincerely thank you for coming along for this second Gold Country adventure. God bless!

Dana Mentink

Get 2 Free Books,
Plus 2 Free Gifts—
just for trying the Reader Service!

Get 2 Free Books,
Plus 2 Free Gifts—
just for trying the Reader Service!

HOME on the RANCH

YES! Please send me the **Home on the Ranch Collection** in Larger Print. This collection begins with 3 FREE books and 2 FREE gifts in the first shipment. Along with my 3 free books, I'll also get the next 4 books from the Home on the Ranch Collection, in LARGER PRINT, which I may either return and owe nothing, or keep for the low price of $5.24 U.S./ $5.89 CDN each plus $2.99 for shipping and handling per shipment*. If I decide to continue, about once a month for 8 months I will get 6 or 7 more books, but will only need to pay for 4. That means 2 or 3 books in every shipment will be FREE! If I decide to keep the entire collection, I'll have paid for only 32 books because 19 books are FREE! I understand that accepting the 3 free books and gifts places me under no obligation to buy anything. I can always return a shipment and cancel at any time. My free books and gifts are mine to keep no matter what I decide.

268 HCN 3760 468 HCN 3760

Name	(PLEASE PRINT)	
Address		Apt. #
City	State/Prov.	Zip/Postal Code

Signature (if under 18, a parent or guardian must sign)

Mail to the **Reader Service:**

IN U.S.A.: P.O. Box 1867, Buffalo, NY. 14240-1867
IN CANADA: P.O. Box 609, Fort Erie, Ontario L2A 5X3

* Terms and prices subject to change without notice. Prices do not include applicable taxes. Sales tax applicable in NY. Canadian residents will be charged applicable taxes. This offer is limited to one order per household. All orders subject to approval. Credit or debit balances in a customer's account(s) may be offset by any other outstanding balance owed by or to the customer. Please allow 3 to 4 weeks for delivery. Offer available while quantities last. Offer not available to Quebec residents.

Your Privacy—The Reader Service is committed to protecting your privacy. Our Privacy Policy is available online at www.ReaderService.com or upon request from the Reader Service.

We make a portion of our mailing list available to reputable third parties that offer products we believe may interest you. If you prefer that we not exchange your name with third parties, or if you wish to clarify or modify your communication preferences, please visit us at www.ReaderService.com/consumerschoice or write to us at Reader Service Preference Service, P.O. Box 9062, Buffalo, NY. 14240-9062. Include your complete name and address.

READERSERVICE.COM

Manage your account online!

- Review your order history
- Manage your payments
- Update your address

We've designed the
Reader Service website
just for you.

Enjoy all the features!

- Discover new series available to you, and read excerpts from any series.
- Respond to mailings and special monthly offers.
- Browse the Bonus Bucks catalog and online-only exculsives.
- Share your feedback.

Visit us at:
ReaderService.com